中国鬼故事 Chinese Ghost Stories

U0109094

The Commercial Press

中国鬼故事

Chinese Ghost Stories

Published by: The Commercial Press (U.S.) Ltd.
The Corporation, 2nd Floor
New York, NY 10013

Chinese Ghost Stories
Intermediate-Advanced Readings in Language and Culture

Author : Edmond Hung, Hon Sun Yu

Editors: Betty WONG, Gladys LEUNG

ISBN: 978 962 07 1888 5
Printed in Hong Kong.

http://www.chinese4fun.net

Contents
目 录

出版说明　Publisher's Note

After studying one to two years of Chinese you have also gained the knowledge of quite a bit of vocabulary. You may be wondering whether there are any other ways for you to further improve your Chinese language proficiency? Although there are a lot of books in the market that are written for people who are studying Chinese it is not easy to find an interesting and easy to read book that matches up to one's level of proficiency. You may find the content and the choice of words for some books to be too difficult to handle. You may also find some books to be too easy and the content is too naive for high school students and adults. Seeing the demand for this kind of learning materials we have designed a series of reading materials, which are composed of vivid and interesting content, presented in a multi-facet format. We think this can help students who are learning Chinese to solve the above problem. Through our reading series you can improve your Chinese and at the same time you will learn a lot of China culture.

Our series includes Chinese culture, social aspects of China, famous Chinese literary excerpts, pictorial symbols of

China, famous Chinese heroes…and many other indispensable aspects of China for those who want to really understand Chinese culture. While enjoying the reading materials one can further one's knowledge of Chinese culture from different angles. The content of the series are contextualized according to the wordbase categorization of HSK. We have selected our diction from the pre-intermediate, intermediate to advanced level of Chinese language learners. Our series is suitable for students at the pre-intermediate, intermediate to advanced level of Chinese and working people who are studying Chinese on their own.

The body of our series is composed of literary articles. The terms used in each article are illustrated with the romanised system called Hànyǔ pīnyīn for the ease in learning the pronunciation. Each article has an English translation with explanation of the vocabulary. Moreover there is related background knowledge in Expansion Reading. Interesting games are added to make it fun to learn. We aim at presenting a three-dimensional study experience of learning Chinese for our readers.

Jié cǎo xián huán
结草衔环
Rope and Jade Rings

Pre-reading Question

1. Rice can be eaten in many ways, not just as cooked rice. Do you know how many food items come from rice?

2. Do you think the belief of "good will be rewarded with good, and evil with evil" is still affecting the Chinese society?

❶
Yǒu yī ge guówáng fēicháng ài
有 一 个 国 王 非 常 爱

tā de niánqīng xiǎolǎopo Yǒu yī
他 的 年 轻 小 老 婆。有 一

cì zhège guówáng shēngbìng le duì
次，这 个 国 王 生 病 了，对

tā de érzi shuō Jiǎrú wǒ
他 的 儿 子 说："假 如 我

sǐ le nǐ yīdìng yào bǎ tā
死 了，你 一 定 要 把 她

jià gěi biéren Hòulái zhège
嫁 给 别 人"。后 来 这 个

guówáng bìng de hěn zhòng lín
国 王 病 得 很 重，临

The King's young mistress

死前 又 对 儿子 说：" 我 死 之后，你 要 让 她 陪 我 死。" 这个 国王 死后，他 儿子 不 忍心 杀死 这个 年轻 的 女人，便 按照 父亲 之前 的 想法，将 她 嫁 给 别人。别人 问 儿子 为什么 这样 做，儿子 说：" 父亲 病 得 很 重 的 时候，是 不 清醒 的。我 把 父亲 的 小老婆 嫁 出去，是 按照 父亲 清醒 时候 的 安排。"

Translation

❶　　A king was very fond of his young mistress. When he was sick, he instructed his son, "If I die, find her another husband," he said. Later, he became gravely sick. "Bury her with me after my death" were his last words to his son. Finding the idea too cruel, his son found another man to marry this young mistress as his father had instructed earlier. His younger brother asked why he did so. "Dad was out of his mind when he was heavily sick. I just followed the instruction given to me when he was clear-headed," he said.

❷

Hòulái érzi chéngwéile jūnguān Yǒu yī cì tā
后来，儿子 成为了 军官。有 一 次，他

shuàilǐng jūnduì zuòzhàn yuè dǎ yuè jīliè jiànjiàn láidào yī
率领 军队 作战，越 打 越 激烈，渐渐 来到 一

piàn zhǎngmǎn zácǎo de xiǎo shān shang Zhè shíhou yī ge
片 长满 杂草 的 小 山 上。这 时候，一 个

lǎorén tūrán chūxiàn lǎorén fēikuài de yòng dì shang de
老人 突然 出现，老人 飞 快 地 用 地 上 的

cǎo biānchéng yī ge yī ge huán ránhòu kànzhǔnle jīhuì jiāng
草 编成 一 个 一 个 环，然后 看准了 机会，将

tā pāo xiàng érzi de dírén dírén yīxiàzi dǎole
它 抛 向 儿子 的 敌人，敌人 一下子 倒了

xiàlái Érzi dǎbàile dírén lìxia gōngláo dédàole
下来。儿子 打败了 敌人，立下 功劳，得到了

hěn duō jiǎngpǐn Nàtiān wǎnshang tā zuòle yī ge
很 多 奖品。那天 晚上，他 做了 一 个

mèng Mèng lǐmiàn báitiān de
梦。梦 里面，白天 的

nàge lǎorén xiàozhe duì
那个 老人 笑着 对

Fighting in a battle

他 说:"你 救过 一个 年轻 的 女人,我 是
那个 女人 的 父亲。我 今天 这样 做,是 为了
报答 你。"

成语"结草衔环"就 是 和 以上 的 故事
相关 的。

Translation

❷   Later, this son became a military commander. One day, he and his troops were at war with an enemy. Battling fiercely, they proceeded to a small hill grown with weeds. At that moment, an old man appeared from nowhere, quickly made a strong rope from the weeds and threw it towards the enemy. Tripped by the rope, the enemy was caught and the son was heavily rewarded for his victory. That night, in his dream, he saw the old man smiling at him. "I am the young mistress's father. What I did today is my reward for your kindness," the old man said.

The Chinese idiom Jiécǎoxiánhuán is related to the above story.

Consequences of Good and Evil

There is a Chinese saying that goes: "Good will be rewarded with good, and evil with evil. The consequences will come sooner or later". They believe that good deeds will be rewarded with a blessing or something good while bad deeds will lead to ill luck or something bad. There will be no exception. From a Buddhist perspective, the consequences of good and evil come as natural as the shadows following our bodies. Wherever we go, we can never get rid of our own shadows.

What is good and what is evil? The standards and definitions have been constantly evolving. Their meanings vary with respect to different people, groups and regions, and change as the society develops. The common understanding is that "good" is something that does more good than harm, while "bad" is something on the contrary. However, many things are intermingled with good and harm; in fact it is not easy to classify them as good or bad in a clear-cut manner.

Another question is, who is responsible for bringing forth the consequences? The Chinese used to say, "All deeds are watched by God from above." They believe that gods and spirits are in charge of the life, death, misfortune and well-being of all human beings; they can even read people's mind. The saying is therefore a warning reminding people and their offspring to suppress their bad thoughts. The gods and spirits are impartial so no one can escape the consequences. Their realization will come in a matter of time.

Tán Shēng

谈生

Tan Sheng

Pre-reading Question

1. Do you think all ghosts in China look ugly?

2. Imagine what would happen if a ghost got married to a human being.

3. Is there any difference between the revival of the dead in Chinese ghost stories and resurrection in foreign movies?

❶
Tán Shēng zhǎng de hǎokàn dàn jiā li hěn qióng suǒyǐ
谈 生 长 得好看，但 家 里 很 穷，所以

dào zhōngnián hái méiyǒu
到 中年 还 没有

jiéhūn Yǒu yī tiān yǐjing
结婚。有一天，已经

shì bànyè le Tán
是 半夜 了， 谈

Shēng háishi zài
生 还是 在

dúshū Zhè
读书。 这

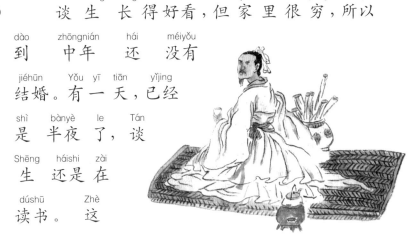

A bachelor in middle age

6

时候，外面传来声音，接着，一位约十几岁的美丽少女走进来。她进来后，朝谈生行了一个礼，然后说："我本来不想打扰你，只是不忍心看到你这么晚了还是在读书，所以进来陪您。"谈生连忙接待这个少女。少女说："我叫阿紫，本来与家里的人一起，现在迷了路。偶然来到你家的门口。看到你用功读书，十分佩服。知道你还没有结婚，如果你不嫌我配不上你，我愿意嫁给你。"说到这里，阿紫的脸已经红了。谈生听了这番话，立即说："姑娘看得起我，我实在感激不尽。我当然也希望能跟姑娘一起生活，永远不分别。"阿紫说："不过，有一件事我先跟你说明。我跟别人不同，从小得了一种病，三年内不能够见

guāng wǎnshang yě bù néng liàng dēng Tán Shēng xiǎng yě
光，晚上也不能亮灯。"谈生想也

méi xiǎng jiù dāying le Jiéhūn hòu tāmen de gǎnqíng hěn
没想就答应了。结婚后，他们的感情很

hǎo Dì èr nián tāmen biàn yǒule yī ge érzi shēnghuó
好。第二年，他们便有了一个儿子，生活

shífēn xìngfú
十分幸福。

Translation

❶   Tan Sheng was handsome but poor. He was still a bachelor in middle age. One night, it was very late and Tan Sheng was reading. There was some noise outside. Then a beautiful young lady came in. "I don't mean to interrupt you. I just saw you studying late at night, so I come in to be your company," she said softly after greeting Tan Sheng.

Tan Sheng invited her to come in the house. "My name is Purple. I came here today with my family but I have lost contact with them. By chance I came across your door. I saw you studying hard and I was very impressed. I would like to be your wife if you don't mind," she said shyly as her cheeks flushed red. Having listened to what she said, Tan Sheng replied quickly, "I am most grateful for your appreciation. It is of course my greatest luck to have you as my lifelong companion."

Purple continued, "But there is one thing that I must tell you beforehand. I have been sick since I was a kid and that made me different. I can't see the light, not even candle light at night for three years."

Tan Sheng committed without a second thought. They had a happy marriage and their son was born in the following year.

❷

不过，谈生有时候会很好奇，为什么阿紫说不能见光呢？终于有一次，他忍不住了，等阿紫睡了，偷偷拿灯来照她，看到可怕的情景。原来阿紫的腰以下，只有骨头，没有肉。阿紫醒来后伤心地说："为什么两年都等过来了，还有一年你不肯等呢？我都快活过来了，现在没办法了，我们再不能一起生活了。"谈生道歉已来不及了。阿紫说："虽然我跟你必须分别，可是我不放心儿子。想到他以后要吃苦，我就很难受。你跟我来，我送你一件东西，如果以后你生活太困难了，就可以拿去卖。"说完后就带谈生来到一间

A lamp

屋 里，里面 的 物品 都 很 特别。阿紫 撕下了
wū li，lǐmiàn de wùpǐn dōu hěn tèbié。Āzǐ sīxiale

谈 生 身 上 的 一 块 布，然后 拿了 一 件
Tán Shēng shēn shang de yī kuài bù，ránhòu nále yī jiàn

衣服 递给 他，说："凭 这 件 衣服，你 生活 就
yīfu dìgěi tā，shuō："Píng zhè jiàn yīfu，nǐ shēnghuó jiù

不 会 再 有 困难。"说完 后 她 和 屋 都 不见
bù huì zài yǒu kùnnan。"Shuōwán hòu tā hé wū dōu bùjiàn

了。
le

Translation

❷   Nevertheless, Tan Sheng was curious about Purple's sickness; why couldn't she not even stand having a candle lit at night? One night, he could not help his curiosity. Quietly, when Purple was asleep, he lit up a lamp and let it light on her. He was extremely terrified by what he saw: down from her waist, she had only bones, no flesh at all!

Purple woke up and said in grief, "You have kept your promise for two years; why can't you keep it for one more year? I can almost live again. Nothing can be done now. We can no longer live together."

Tan Sheng apologized but it was too late. "Though we must separate, I love our son. As a mother, I can't stand the thought that he may suffer in the future. Come with me, I have something for you. You can sell it at difficult times," said Purple.

Purple led Tan Sheng to a house in which everything seemed unusual. She tore a piece from Tan Sheng's clothing, then handed him a robe. "You can be self-sufficient with this," she said before vanishing with the house.

❸ 几年后，谈生十分穷，便拿那件衣服去卖，结果有一个仆人用很高的价钱买了。衣服拿回去后，那个富有的主人奇怪地说："这不是我女儿的衣服吗？卖它的人肯定是从墓里偷来的，快抓住他。"谈生被抓后，将事情告诉那个主人。他最初不相信，还叫人打开女儿的墓，发现墓里的物品没有被人动过。女儿的身边还放着一块布，就是阿紫从谈生身上撕下来的那块布。那个主人又看到谈生的儿子跟自己的女儿长得很像，终于相信谈生是女儿的丈夫。后来，他为谈生的儿子请来最好的老师，让他接受最好的教育。谈生的儿子长大后在政府当了大官。

Translation

❸   A few years later, Tan Sheng sold the robe when he was in extreme poverty. The buyer was a servant of a king. The king was stunned when he saw the robe. "Isn't this my daughter's robe? The one who sold it must have stolen it from the tomb, catch him," he ordered.

Tan Sheng was caught and he told the king everything but he was unconvinced. The king gave orders to break open the tomb and found that things inside were totally intact. Strange though, a piece of cloth was found beside his daughter. It was exactly the piece of cloth that Purple torn from Tan Sheng. The king was also surprised by Tan Sheng's son, who look like his daughter. That made him finally believed that Tan Sheng was his daughter's husband. With the king's help, Tan Sheng's son grew up with quality education from the best teachers and became a senior government official.

Female Ghosts and Revival of the Dead

According to Chinese custom, the spirit of the deceased will return on the seventh day after death (so-called the returning night). The spirit will return home and bid farewell to its family (not face to face, but quietly) for the final time. It will then drink the "soup of forgetfulness" and set for rebirth. On the returning night, the family of the deceased will prepare plenty of tributes to treat the dead and the ghost messengers who will be responsible for taking the deceased to hell. If the spirit of the deceased does not return home that day, the ghost messengers cannot take it to hell. It will end up as a wandering ghost belonging to nowhere.

In fact, revival of the dead is common in Chinese stories. However, it is different from the idea of resurrecting for vengeance, which is common in foreign movies. In the Chinese context, it is usually about young women who became ghosts after losing their lives for different reasons. As the stories develop, they are revived and manage to live with their lovers happily ever after.

"*The Peony Pavilion*" is a classical example of these stories. A young lady Du Liniang fell in love with a man she had dreamed about. She died for her love and became a ghost. After death, she met her dreamed lover. With her persistence, she was given a second life that enabled her to marry her lover in the real world. Like Du Liniang, almost all female ghosts were shown to be courageous for the sake of love in Chinese stories about revival of the dead. They dared to fight with people and fate; they died and relived for the love they had dreamed about and had pursued for. It is no wonder that when talking with a Chinese person about female ghosts and revival of the dead, he or she would spontaneously relate to tragic and touching love stories instead of scary murders or killings.

GAMES FOR FUN

Can you identify which picture is not a Chinese tomb?

(1)

(2)

(3)

(4)

Zǐyù

紫玉

Ziyu

Pre-reading Question

1. In ancient China, parents had great authority over their children's marriage. Do you think such parental influence still exists in China?

2. Have you ever seen a wedding between a man and a female ghost in Chinese movies?

Yī ge niánqīngrén zài mù qián hěn shāngxīn de kū
一 个 年 轻 人 在 墓 前 很 伤 心 地 哭。

Zhège niánqīngrén jiào Hán Zhòng Mù li tǎngzhe tā
这 个 年 轻 人 叫 韩 重。 墓 里 躺 着 他

de àiren Zǐyù Hán Zhòng fēicháng yǒu xuéwen ér
的 爱 人 —— 紫 玉。 韩 重 非 常 有 学 问，而

Zǐyù jiù měilì dòngrén Tāmen tōutōu de xǐhuan
紫 玉 就 美 丽 动 人。 他 们 偷 偷 地 喜 欢

duìfāng hǎojiǔ le Dàn Zǐyù shì yī ge wáng de xiǎo
对 方 好 久 了。 但 紫 玉 是 一 个 王 的 小

nǚ'ér ér Hán Zhòng zhǐshì gōng li yī ge pǔtōng de xiǎo
女 儿，而 韩 重 只 是 宫 里 一 个 普 通 的 小

官员，他们即使喜欢对方，也只能够偷偷地以书信往来。

　　三年前，韩重准备出国读书，寻找更好的发展机会。临走之前，紫玉请求韩重向父亲提出结婚。紫玉的父亲看到地位低的韩重竟然想娶自己最疼爱的女儿，不同意这婚姻。紫玉知道后，十分伤心，不久便生病死了。三年后，韩重回来知道紫玉死了，非常难过，便在她的墓前大哭。

A tomb

Translation

❶   In front of the grave, a young man was mourning in deep grief. Tears kept running down his face.

His name was Han Zhong. Inside the tomb laid his lover Ziyu. Han Zhong was a brilliant young man, and Ziyu was a charming young lady. They secretly fell in love with each other for a long time. Unfortunately, Ziyu was the king's youngest daughter while Han Zhong was only a junior official serving in the palace. Their love could only be secretly communicated through letters.

Three years ago, Han Zhong left for better opportunities in another country. Before his departure, Ziyu asked Han Zhong to have his parents propose their marriage to the king . In the king's eyes, Han Zhong was completely a nobody. How dare him to dream of marrying his beloved daughter! He turned down the proposal. Ziyu was very sad and not long afterwards, she died of illness. Three years later, Han Zhong returned home only to find that Ziyu was dead and this is where the story unfolds.

❷ 也许 是 韩 重 的 眼泪 感动了 天，紫玉 的 鬼魂 从 墓 里 走 出来，对 韩 重 说："想不到 三 年 前 的 分别 变成了 永远 的 分别。三 年 了，我 终于 等到 你 了，你 知道 我 有 多 想 你 吗？这 三 年 里，我 感到 很 寂寞 啊。今天，你 终于 回来 了，你 能 陪 我 吗？"韩 重 虽然 也 思念 紫玉，但 他 还是 很 害怕："你 是 鬼，我 是 人，就 像 走 在 不 同 的 路 上，我 不 能 接受 你 的 邀请。"紫玉 说："我 知道 我们 人 鬼 有别，可是，这 次 分别 后，我们 什么 时候 才 能够 再见 呢？"紫玉 伸出了 手，韩 重 没有 再 拒绝，跟着 她 进了 墓 里面。三 年 未 见，他们 互相 表达 思念 之 苦，并 正式

A pearl necklace

jiéwéi fūqī Sān tiān hòu Hán Zhòng yào zǒu le Zǐyù
结为 夫妻。 三 天 后， 韩 重 要 走 了。 紫玉

qǔchu yī kē zhēnzhū sònggěi Hán Zhòng duì tā shuō Cóng
取出 一 颗 珍珠， 送给 韩 重 ， 对 他 说："从

xiànzài qǐ qǐng zhàogù hǎo zìjǐ Rúguǒ dàole gōng
现在 起， 请 照顾 好 自己。 如果 到 了 宫

li qǐng dài wǒ xiàng fùqin wènhǎo
里， 请 代 我 向 父亲 问好。"

Translation

❷   Han Zhong's tears might have moved the heavenly gods. Ziyu's ghost came out from the tomb and said to Han Zhong, "How come does the farewell that was three years ago turned out to be a goodbye that lasted forever? I have been waiting for three years and you finally came. Do you know how much I have missed you?"

Ziyu said, "I was so lonely during these last three years. Now you are back, can you be my company?" Though Han Zhong also missed Ziyu very much, he was afraid and said, "You are a ghost and I am a man, we are heading for different roads, I cannot accept your invitation."

"I see. Yet, if you leave me this time, when we will meet again?" she sighed.

Ziyu reached out her hand. Han Zhong no longer refused and followed her into the tomb. They shared all the bitterness and thoughts from the last three years and they became husband and wife.

After three days, Han Zhong had to go. Ziyu gave him a pearl as a gift. "From now on, please take care of yourself. When you go back to the palace, please send my regards to my father," she said.

❸ 韩重回到宫里，拿着珍珠去见紫玉的父亲，提起和他女儿见面的事。她父亲很生气，说他在墓里偷东西，还命令士兵捉他。韩重逃到紫玉墓前，告诉她这件事。紫玉说："不要担心，今天我就回去见父亲。"她父亲正在宫中生气，看见女儿进来，大吃一惊，又高兴，又难过。紫玉跪下来说："以前韩重的父母来提出结婚，父亲不同意，我伤心而死。韩重从远处回来，听说我死了，所以到墓前看我，我被他的深情感动，出来和他见面，并送给他珍珠，那颗珍珠并不是他挖墓偷取的。希望父亲答应女儿，不要再捉韩重了。"紫玉的父亲知道了女儿的心意，也不再捉韩重了。

Translation

❸ Han Zhong returned to the palace and told the king about his reunion with Ziyu. The king was very angry and condemned Han Zhong for having raided the tomb. The king ordered Han Zhong to be arrested. Han Zhong escaped. He ran to Ziyu's grave and told her what had happened. "Don't worry, I will go back and explain to the King today," said Ziyu.

In the palace, the king was still angry. When he saw his daughter, he was shocked, very pleased but also sad. Ziyu kneeled and begged, "Dad, when Han Zhong's parents came with the marriage proposal, you turned it down. In huge disappointment, I died. Han Zhong returned and had learnt about my death. He visited my grave. Moved by his deep love, I met with him and gave him the pearl. It wasn't stolen. Han Zhong is innocent. Dad, please promise me that you will not arrest him."

The king respected Ziyu's wish and withdrew the order to arrest Han Zhong.

Yin and Yang – Worlds for the Dead and the Alive

The Chinese believe that Yin and Yang are two different worlds for the dead and the alive. "Death" has the implication of "return" which means returning to the world before birth. People become "ghosts" after death, and "ghost" also signifies "return". Human beings are born with souls. When one dies, his body finally returns to dust and earth. Yet his soul will leave the body, drifts around and remains in this state forever. The living people inhabit in the world of Yang. After death, they will inhabit in the world of Yin in the form of "ghosts".

All these beliefs reflect the Chinese's desire to bridge "life" and "death" as a way of minimizing people's fear about death.

This explains why the Chinese people have complicated burial ceremonies and rituals. They believe that rituals like burning bundles of "underworld money", preparing plenty of offerings, choosing the site of a tomb according to Feng Shui, and providing a nice, comfortable "residence" for the dead can ensure that the deceased will live well in the world of Yin. Moreover, many believe that the deceased may become powerful ghosts or spirits who can protect their offspring from misfortune and bless them with wealth and good luck.

Of the various Chinese festivals connected with gods and ghosts of worship, the Qing Ming Festival is a popular one. It is the day when people show their respect and retrospect for the deceased by visiting the graves to clean up the site, burn "underworld money", decorate with some fresh green branches and make offerings of wine and fruit.

GAMES FOR FUN

Offering ceremonial sacrifices is a Chinese custom. Which of the following things are used in such ceremony nowadays?

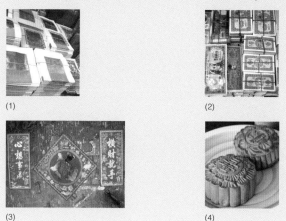

(1)   (2)

(3)   (4)

Dìngbó mài guǐ

定伯卖鬼

Dingbo Sold the Ghost

Pre-reading Question

1. Is it possible for a man to deceive a ghost? What do you think?

2. Can you guess what can scare away ghosts?

---

❶

Yǒu yī ge jiào Sòng Dìngbó de rén dǎn tèbié
有 一 个 叫 宋 定伯 的 人，胆 特别

dà rénmen chēng tā wéi Sòng Dàdǎn Yǒu yī cì tā
大，人们 称 他 为 "宋 大胆"。有 一 次 他

wǎnshang zài lù shang yùdào yī ge rén tā wèn Nǐ
晚上 在 路 上 遇到 一 个 人，他 问："你

shì shuí Nà rén dá Wǒ shì guǐ Sòng Dìngbó hěn
是 谁？" 那 人 答："我 是 鬼。" 宋 定伯 很

qíguài zǐxì kàn nàge guǐ de yàngzi hěn nánkàn Guǐ
奇怪，仔细 看，那个 鬼 的 样子 很 难看。 鬼

wèn tā Nǐ yòu shì shuí Sòng Dìngbó piàn tā shuō Wǒ
问 他："你 又 是 谁？" 宋 定伯 骗 他 说："我

yě shì guǐ Guǐ wèn tā Nǐ yào qù nǎli Sòng
也 是 鬼。" 鬼 问 他："你 要 去 哪里？" 宋

Dìngbó shuō Wǒ yào qù shìchǎng Guǐ shuō Wǒ yě
定伯 说："我 要 去 市场。" 鬼 说："我 也

要去 那里，我们 一起 走 吧。" 宋 定伯 胆
虽然 大，但是 晚上 跟 鬼 一起 还是 有些
害怕。 不过 他 冷静 下来，决定 先 答应
鬼，然后 再 想 办法。

Translation

❶   Song Dingbo, nicknamed "Courageous Song", was a man with exceptional bravery. One day, he met a man when traveling late at night. He asked, "Who are you?" The man answered, "Ghost."

Startled, Song Dingbo looked carefully at the man and he saw a ghostly and ugly face. "Who are you then?" asked the ghost.

"I am a ghost too," Song Dingbo lied.

"Where are you heading for?"

"The market," said Song Dingbo. "I am going to the market too. Let's go together," said the ghost.

Though Song Dingbo was fearless, the idea of traveling with a ghost during the middle of the night scared him a little. Nevertheless, he reminded himself to keep cool and it was better for him to accept the invitation first and see how things go.

❷ 走了 不久，鬼 说："这样 走 太 慢 了 吧，我们 互相 背着 走，怎么样？"宋 定伯 说："这个 主意 不错，你 先 背 我 吧。"于是 鬼 背着 他，说："你 怎么 这样 重 的？ 你 到底 是不是 鬼 啊？"宋 定伯 赶紧 回答："我 当然 是 鬼 了，不过 我 才 死了 不久，还是 新 的 鬼，所以 有些 重 啊。"鬼 听了 没 再 说 什么。过了 不久，换 宋 定伯 背 鬼 了，鬼 果然 很 轻，像 是 没有 重量 一样。 他们 轮流 互相 背着 走 许多 次。 宋 定伯 问 鬼："我 现在 还是 新 的 鬼，不 知道 我们 鬼 有些 什么 害怕 的 事情 呢？"鬼 回答 说："最 怕 人 吐 口水。"过了 一会，前面 出现 一 条 河。宋 定伯 叫 鬼 先 过去，鬼 过去 的 时候，静 得 一些 声音 也 没有。到 宋 定伯 过去 的 时候，发出 哇啦哇啦 的 声音。 又

yǐnqǐ guǐ de huáiyí　Wèishénme nǐ huì nòngchu zhème
引起 鬼 的 怀疑:"为什么 你 会 弄出 这么

dà de shēngyīn ne　Sòng Dìngbó liánmáng huídá Wǒ gāng
大 的 声音 呢?"宋 定伯 连忙 回答:"我 刚

sǐ hái méi dùguo shuǐ yǒu yīxiē bù xíguàn
死,还 没 渡过 水,有 一些 不 习惯。"

Translation

❷　After a while, the ghost said, "Walking is too slow. How about we take turns carrying each other?"

"This is a good idea. You carry me first," said Song Dingbo.

The ghost carried Song Dingbo on its back and grumbled, "Are you really a ghost? How can you be so heavy?" "Of course I am. It's because I recently died, so I am still a bit heavy," Song Dingbo quickly made up a reason and the ghost said no more.

Then it was Song Dingbo's turn. He carried the ghost who was as light as air.

In this way, they took turns carrying each other. Song Dingbo asked, "As a ghost, I am still new. Do you know anything that we ghosts are usually afraid of?" "It differs. For me, I am most afraid of people spitting," said the ghost.

A moment later they came to a river.

Song Dingbo let the ghost cross the river first. It went quietly without any sound. When it came to Song Dingbo's turn, he crossed with loud splashes. "Why did you make so much noise?" the ghost turned suspicious again. Song Dingbo explained at once, "I am a recent dead. This is my first time crossing a river in the form of ghost. I haven't gotten used to this."

3

他们 赶了 很 远 的 路，天 也 快 亮
了，市场 就 在 前面。这 时候，宋 定伯 背
鬼，他 用力 抓住 鬼 很快 地 往 前面 跑。鬼
一边 大声 叫，一边 要求 宋 定伯 把 它 放
下来。宋 定伯 不 听，一直 抓紧 它，背
到 市场 中，然后 才 放 在 地 上。鬼
立即 变成 一 头 羊 的 样子。宋 定伯
怕 它 再 有 变化，连忙 向 它 吐了 一 口
口水。后来，陆续 有 人 来 看 这 头 羊，宋
定伯 就 卖了 羊，得到 一千 五百 元。后来
大家 就 说："宋 大胆 卖 鬼，得 钱 一千
五百"。

A goat

Translation

❸   They traveled a long way till daybreak and the market was near. At this moment, Song Dingbo grabbed the ghost unexpectedly and carried it on his shoulders. Then he ran as quickly as he could. The ghost yelled loudly and wanted Song Dingbo to put it down. Yet Song Dingbo turned a deaf ear to its words. He let down the ghost only when he reached the middle of the market. The ghost immediately turned into a goat. Fearing that it would turn into something else, Song Dingbo spat at it. Then, the goat attracted attention from some of those in the market and Song Dingbo got it sold. It was said that "Courageous Song sold the ghost for one thousand and five hundred bucks" and the story became popular.

Chinese Ghosts

All countries and regions have their own understanding and imagination with respect to ghosts. The images of ghosts differ greatly between the West and the East. For the West, their ghosts are mostly vampires, werewolves, zombies and headless riders, whereas the ghosts of the East are mainly pale, sad ladies with long hair. The western ghosts are dominantly horrible and bloody males while the eastern ghosts are usually kind-hearted or bitter, and are mostly females and children.

The western ghosts are tangible while the eastern ghosts are intangible and drift around. Under the eastern culture, ghost is like a shadow of the deceased, it carries the appearance of the deceased before death. In Chinese communities, it is widely believed when one dies, his soul will become ghost. Aging, illness and death are things out of man's

A modern market

control and some natural phenomena are beyond people's comprehension. The belief that the deceased will head for another world and the concept of ghosts were thus formulated.

The ghosts have little but weak supernatural powers. Usually, they only belong to the underworld. Occasionally, some ghosts may wander into this world and are unwilling to leave due to unaccomplished issues or unfulfilled wishes. Of course, these kinds of actions are forbidden in hell and these ghosts will be severely punished. When the ghosts are in the world of the living, they are relatively weak and can only come out at night. They can only scare people and are unable to do anything really harmful.

For ghosts, there are usually three outcomes. The first and also the most common one is to reincarnate into human beings or other creatures depending on their virtue before death. The second one is to be tortured in hell and this is mainly for those who committed a lot of sins before death. The third and also a very unusual one is to transcend to be a god. In general, only those with remarkable virtue or influence before death may be picked by heaven to carry out specific duties. For example, Judge Bao was assigned to be the King of Hell after his death.

GAMES FOR FUN

The Chinese believe that certain things can overpower evil influence. Choose the right items from below.

(1)

(2)

(3)

(4)

Zhōng Kuí zhuō guǐ

钟馗捉鬼

Zhong Kui, the Ghost Catcher

Zhong Kui

Pre-reading Question

1. Do you put up pictures on your door? Do they have any special meaning?

2. Have you ever seen any door gods in China? Do they look frightening?

---

❶
Xīnnián de shíhou měi jiā de ménkǒu dōu guàzhe yī
新年 的 时候，每 家 的 门口 都 挂着 一

fú huà huà zhōng yǒu yī ge tóu xiàng lǎohǔ yuán yǎn tiě
幅 画，画 中 有 一 个 头 像 老虎、圆 眼、铁

liǎn zhǎng húzi de rén yàngzi nánkàn de bùdéliǎo Tā
脸、长 胡子 的 人，样子 难看 得 不得了。他

jiùshì zhuānmén tì huángdì zhuā guǐ de Zhong Kuí
就是 专门 替 皇帝 抓 鬼 的 钟 馗。

Translation

❶ In the Chinese Lunar New Year, every household puts up a picture. In this picture, an ugly person has a tiger-like head and big round eyes, wearing a long moustache with grim facial expression. He is Zhong Kui, the famous ghost catcher for the Emperor.

❷ 传说 有 一 个 皇帝，病 了 一 个
多 月，没 有 一 个 医生 能 治好 他。一天
夜里，皇帝 发烧，梦见 一 个 小鬼 走 进
大殿，他 长着 牛 鼻子，穿着 红 衣服 和 一
只 鞋，腰 上 挂着 一 只 鞋，脖子 后面 还
插着 一 把 纸 扇子。他 竟然 偷 皇帝 的
笛子，皇帝 很 生气，刚 要 叫 人 抓 小鬼，这
时候 突然 跑 出来 一 个 大 鬼。这个 大 鬼
穿 蓝 衣服，一 个 胳膊 露 在 外面，头发
零乱，胡子 长长 的，样子 长 得 极其
可怕。大 鬼 追 上去 抓住 小鬼，挖掉 他
的 眼睛，一口 吞 了。皇帝 吓坏 了，赶快
问："你 是 谁？为什么 帮 我 抓 小鬼？"大
鬼 回答："我 叫 钟 馗。前 几 年 曾经 考
得 第一 名，成绩 很 好，可是 负责 考试 的
官 看 我 的 样子 太 丑 了，就 故意 改了 我

的 成绩，让 我 没 办法 为 皇帝 您 服务！我
一 生气，当 他们 的 面 就 头 撞 柱子，结果
撞死 了。现在 我 做了 鬼，愿意 为 皇帝
服务，我 愿意 为 您 捉鬼！"他 说话 的 声音
很 大，一下子 把 皇帝 吓 醒 了，出了 一 身
的 冷汗，病 也 就 好 了。

An Emperor

Translation

❷   According to the legend, an Emperor fell ill for a month. None of the doctors can cure him of the disease.

One night, the Emperor had a fever and he dreamt of a little demon sneaking into the palace. The little demon had a cow's nose. Dressed in red, he wore one shoe and the other shoe was hanging on his waist. He had a paper fan at the back of his neck. All of a sudden, he snatched the Emperor's bamboo flute. The Emperor was furious and summoned attendants to catch the thief. At this moment, a big demon came out from the back chamber of the palace. Dressed in blue with bare arms, the big demon had a fearsome appearance with untidy long hair and long moustache. The big demon grasped the little demon, pulled out its eyes and swallowed them down. The Emperor was very scared. He asked the big demon, "Who are you? Why did you catch the thief for me?" The big demon replied, "My name is Zhong Kui. In previous years, I achieved good results in the government official exam. But since the examiner felt that my appearance was too ugly and horrifying, he deliberately failed me in the exam so that I could not serve you, my majesty. I was so angry that I smashed my head against a pillar and I died. Now I have become a ghost and I am willing to serve you, my majesty. I am willing to catch ghosts for you." Zhong Kui's voice was loud and awoke the Emperor from his dream. He sweated profusely and his sickness was cured without the use of any medicine.

❸

皇帝 非常 高兴，马上 请 有名 的 画家
到 宫 里，把 夜里 的 梦 告诉 他，请 他 画
一 幅 画。画家 好像 自己 看过 一样，很 快
画 好 了。皇帝 看到 这 幅 画 以后，十分
奇怪，问 画家："难道 你 也 做了 跟 我 一样
的 梦 吗？怎么 能 画 得 这么 像？"画家
说："是的！我 也 做了 这样 的 梦，可是
这个 梦 对 您 来说 是 好 的 事情。您
看，现在 果然 有 一 个 大 鬼 来 保卫
皇帝 了。请 放心，这 表示 您 能 统治 好
国家！"后来，皇帝 顺利 地 统治 国家，并且
把 钟 馗 的 像 发 给 老百姓，让 大家 在
除夕 的 时候 贴 在 门 上 赶 鬼。

Translation

❸   The Emperor was very pleased and he summoned a famous painter to the palace. The Emperor told the painter about the dream and asked him to paint a picture. The painter painted as if he had really seen Zhong Kui and he finished the picture very quickly. The Emperor was astonished when he saw the picture. He asked the painter, "Have you got the same dream as mine? How could you paint Zhong Kui just like the real person? The painter said, "Yes, I have had the same dream as yours. But this dream is good for you, my majesty. Look, a big demon would come to protect you. Please be rest assured. This is a good sign for you to rule the country!"

Later, the Emperor ran the country very well. He ordered officials to have the painter's picture of Zhong Kui reproduced and delivered to all civilians. They could put up the pictures on their doors on the eve of the Chinese Lunar New Year and scare away ghosts.

King of Hell (Yan Wang)

According to Chinese legends, the King of Hell rules over the netherworld and he is in charge of the life and death of man and reincarnation. There is a belief that everyone has to go to the netherworld and undergo judgment by the King of Hell. Yan Wang has a book of life and death that records each person's lifespan. When a person is destined to die, Yan Wang will order his generals Bai Wuchang and Hei Wuchang to bring the person's soul to the netherworld to face judgment. Yan Wang will judge according to this person's good or bad deeds. Yan Wang can reward a person's good deeds by appointing him to become a god or giving him a prosperous next life while he can punish a person's bad deeds by keeping him in the hell or giving him a poor next life. This reflects the Chinese belief of "good will be rewarded with good, and evil with evil".

In the Song dynasty, there was a famous judge called Bao Zheng. He was a symbol of righteousness. According to Chinese legends, he has become the King of Hell after his death and he went on playing the role of a judge. Some legends even say that he is judging humans in daylight and ghosts at night.

GAMES FOR FUN

According to Chinese legends, the following people are King of Hell's generals. Can you guess their job duties?

(1) Niutou Mamian 牛头马面

(2) Heibaiwuchang 黑白无常

(3) Gui zu 鬼卒

Answer:
(1) help Yan Wang judge the reincarnation of man by rewarding the good and punishing the evil.
(2) bring a person's soul to the netherworld after the person's death.
(3) run errands for the King of Hell.

包公审乌盆

Bāogōng shěn wū pén

Baogong Judges the Black Basin

Pre-reading Question

1. Baogong was known for his admirable character and good deeds. Can you think of any other historical figure who has become a god in Chinese legends?

2. Have you ever watched any Chinese TV programs or movies about Baogong?

---

❶

Diànshì li jīngcháng jiàndào
电视 里 经常 见到

yī ge é shang yǒu yī
一 个 额 上 有 一

dào wān yuè liǎn hěn
道 弯 月, 脸 很

hēi de nánzǐ Tā
黑 的 男子。 他

jiàozuò Bāogōng shì
叫做 包公, 是

gǔdài yī ge yǒumíng
古代 一 个 有名

Baogong in court

的法官。以下是他处理的其中一件有名案件。有一个老人喜欢打抱不平。有一天，他突然想到三年前赵大借了他的钱没有还。他想，今天既然没事做，不如到赵大那里走一趟。老人来赵大的家，忽然发现他家的门口比以前新了，漂亮了，赵大非常快还了钱；老人放好了钱，说："我上了年纪，晚上经常去厕所。你家有许多盆，不如送我一个小的，当作是利息。以后我们谁也不欠谁的了。"赵大说："好啊！你自己挑一个吧。"老人挑了一个不错的小盆，就回家去了。他一边走一边想，平时赵大最爱欠别人的钱，他是靠什么方法赚到钱的呢？

Translation

❶   In the Chinese TV program, we can often see a black-faced tall stout man with a crescent on his forehead. He is Baogong and he worked as a judge. Below was one of his cases.

There was once an old man who was always ready to intervene on behalf of those who were too weak to protect themselves. One day, he had nothing to do and he remembered the money he lent to Zhao Da. Since he was free at the moment, why not visited Zhao Da's home? The old man arrived at Zhao Da's home and found that Zhao Da's home was renovated. Zhao Da returned the money to the old man without any hesitation. The old man took the money and said, "I am an elderly man and I need to go to the washroom very often. Your home has lots of black basins. Could you give me a small one as the interest? Then you don't owe me anything." Zhao Da said, "No problem! You choose one for yourself." The old man chose a small one and brought it home. He walked and thought to himself why Zhao Da had become so generous today. Zhao Da used to owe other people's money. How had he become so rich?

❷ 一天 夜里，老人 在 睡梦 中 听见 有人 叫："你 为什么 往 我 口 中 小便 呢？"他 找了 半天，才 找到 是 那个 乌黑色 的 盆 在 讲话。老人 说："你 告诉 我 发生了 什么 事，我 会 帮 你 的。"乌盆 说："我 是 做 生意 的。因为 行李 过重，借 赵 大 的 家 住了 一 个 晚上。谁 知道 他 和 妻子 都 是 坏人，看中了 我 买 货 的 金，就 把 我 杀死，还 把 我 的 血、肉、骨头 跟 泥 和 起来 做了 盆。希望 你 替 我 找 包公 处理！"第二 天 老人 带着 盆 找 包公，把 赵 大 夫妻 杀人 的 事情 都 告诉 包公。包公 派 人 问 乌 盆，乌 盆 连 一 句 话 也 没 回答，包公 只好 叫 老人 把 盆 带 回去。老人 很 生气，乌 盆 夜里 对 老人 说："今天 因为 没有 衣服，这 事 没 办法

<table>
<tr><td>jiěshì</td><td></td><td>Dì-èr</td><td>tiān</td><td>lǎorén</td></tr>
<tr><td>解释</td><td>。" 第</td><td>二</td><td>天，</td><td>老人</td></tr>
</table>

yòng	yīfu	gěi	pén	gài	hǎo	wū
用	衣服	给	盆	盖	好，	乌

pén	gàosu	le	Bāogōng	yīqiè
盆	告诉	了	包公	一切 。

A black basin

Translation

❷   One night, the old man heard someone screaming, "Why are you pissing into my mouth?" He tried to find where the voice came from. He found that it was the black basin who was talking. The old man said, "Please tell me what happened. I will certainly help you." The black basin said, "I am a businessman. As my luggage was too heavy, I asked Zhao Da for one night's lodging, not knowing that Zhao Da and his wife were bad guys. They murdered me for the gold I had with me and mixed my blood and muscle with clay to make the black basin. I hope you could ask Baogong to handle my case!" On the following day, the old man brought the basin to Baogong and reported how Zhao Da and his wife had committed murder. Baogong asked his official to question the black basin. But it did not utter a word. Baogong had to ask the old man to bring it back home. The old man was very annoyed. The black basin cried to the old man at night, "I could not explain the case because I was not covered with a piece of clothing." On the following day, the old man covered the basin with a piece of clothing and the basin told Baogong the whole story.

❸ 三天以后，包公安排两个助手把赵大和妻子半夜商量杀人的对话重复了一遍，两人吓得要死，可是还不承认。于是把他们都关进监狱，分别查问。包公先对赵大的妻子说："你们杀了人，抢走一百两金，还把他烧成灰，和着泥做了乌盆。分明是你负责藏金的，你丈夫都承认了，你还不承认吗？"赵大妻子信以为真，便带包公把金取出来。在一百两金的面前，赵大只好承认是自己做的，最后包公判了两个人死刑。包公一生处理过无数的案件，受许多人欢迎，大家都叫他"包青天"，说他像头上的青天那么光明。

Translation

❸   Three days later, Baogong asked two assistants to repeat the dialogue to Zhao Da and his wife. Both of them were scared to death but they did not confess. Thus, Baogong put them into prison and interrogated them separately. First, Baogong interrogated Zhao Da's wife, "You and your husband murdered a businessman and seized a hundred taels of gold from him. You also burnt the corpse, mixed the ashes with clay and made the black basin. It was obvious that you were the one who hid the stolen gold. Your husband had already admitted the whole thing, how dare of you not to confess? Zhao Da's wife was tricked into believing that her husband had made the confession and she led Baogong to recover the stolen gold. Seeing the stolen gold, Zhao Da had to confess and finally Baogong passed a death sentence on them.

Having handled numerous cases, Baogong was popular among the people and his popularity earned him a household name "Baoqingtian".

Baogong

Bao Zheng was born in Song dynasty. He was the apple of his parents' eye and he was a filial son. He passed the government exam at the age of 29 and he became an official. Having overcome a great deal of difficulties, he was promoted to the position of vice prime minister.

Baogong was famous for his justice. He was a man of integrity and he would speak the truth even though sometimes it would offend the Emperor. He was good in investigation and ready to listen to other people's opinions. Though Baogong was a high-ranking official, he had a frugal life style just like any of the civilians. He left nothing for his descendants except for a piece of stone on which mottos of anti-corruption was carved. That explained Baogong's popularity among civilians. Many novels, Chinese dramas, literature and TV programs were based on Baogong's stories. Some of the famous stories were *Limao*(狸猫) *Huan Taizi*, *The Wu Pen Case* and *Case of Condemning Chen Shi Mei to Death*.

GAMES FOR FUN

Read the following description and draw a picture of Baogong.

According to the Chinese legend, *Baogong* was not handsome. His face was black in color and there was a crescent on his forehead.

Wèihǔzuòchāng

为虎作伥

The Tiger's Minion

A tiger

Pre-reading Question

1. If a person were bitten to death by a tiger, he would become a ghost according to Chinese superstitions. Can you guess what this ghost would do for the tiger?

2. "Tì Sǐ Guǐ" (scapegoat) has become part of the everyday language in China. Do you know when this expression will be used?

1

Gǔdài de rén bǐjiào míxìn, rènwéi gěi lǎohǔ
古代 的 人 比较 迷信，认为 给 老虎

chīdiào de rén huì biànchéng guǐ, pǎo chulai bāngzhù lǎohǔ
吃掉 的 人 会 变成 鬼，跑 出来 帮助 老虎

shāngrén, zhè zhǒng guǐ jiàozuò "chāngguǐ". Cóngqián, zài yī
伤人，这 种 鬼 叫做 "伥鬼"。从前，在 一

zuò shān shang, měitiān dōu yǒu yī tóu jùdà de xiōng'è de
座 山 上，每天 都 有 一 头 巨大 的、凶恶 的

lǎohǔ shǒu zài fùjìn. Yǒu yī cì, tā méiyǒu zhǎodào
老虎 守 在 附近。有 一 次，它 没有 找到

shíwù, juéde fēicháng nánshòu, tā zài shān shang dàochù
食物，觉得 非常 难受，它 在 山 上 到处

44

寻找 食物。过了 不久，老虎 看见 一 个 很
xúnzhǎo shíwù Guòle bùjiǔ lǎohǔ kànjian yī ge hěn
瘦 的 男人 正在 山 上 走。老虎 想:"虽然
shòu de nánrén zhèngzài shān shang zǒu Lǎohǔ xiǎng Suīrán
这个 人 瘦了 一些，肉 不 多，但 现在 肚子
zhège rén shòule yīxiē ròu bù duō dàn xiànzài dùzi
饿 了，没 办法，这样 瘦 的 肉 也 要 吃
è le méi bànfǎ zhèyàng shòu de ròu yě yào chī
啊。"于是，老虎 在 一 棵 大树 的 后面
a Yúshì lǎohǔ zài yī kē dàshù de hòumian
等着，那个 男人 走近 的 时候，便 扑 过去
děngzhe nàge nánrén zǒujìn de shíhou biàn pū guoqu
吃掉 那个 人。
chīdiào nàge rén

Translation

❶　According to the superstitions of ancient China, it is believed that when a person is bitten to death by a tiger, his ghost will come out to help the tiger assault other people. People call this type of ghost to be a "minion ghost".

In the past, up in the mountains, there was a huge and ferocious tiger that would appear every day. On one occasion, the tiger was starving because it was unable to find any food. As a result, it wandered around everywhere in the mountains in search of food. After a while, the tiger saw in front of it a slim man traveling in the mountains. The tiger thought, "Although this man is a bit slim and does not have much meat, I am too hungry now; I have no choice but to eat such lean meat." As a result, the tiger lurked behind a big tree. When the man approached, the tiger jumped out. The man was bitten to death and his meat was eaten clean.

❷

但是，老虎还没有饱，怎么办呢？这时候，它看见那个男人的魂飘在空中，便抓住那个人的魂。魂说："你吃了我，还要我怎么样呢？"老虎说："你太瘦了，我还不饱。你要帮我多找一个人来吃，否则我不会放你走。你做了鬼，还是一样不自由。相反，你帮了我，不但可以获得自由，以后还可以跟着我干。"魂想："今天我很惨，被老虎吃了。但是，为什么惨事就得落在我的头上？我也要找一个人，让他试一试被老虎吃掉的苦。老虎这么凶，如果我找不到第二个人给它，它也不会放我走呀。"这样一想，魂就同意替老虎找食物了。

Translation

❷   However, the tiger was not full yet. What could it do? At this time, it saw the man's ghost floating into the air; it seized the man's ghost and refused to let it go. The ghost said: "I have already became the food in your belly. What else do you want from me?" The tiger said, "You are too slim and I am not full. You must help me look for a person to fill my stomach; otherwise, I will not let you go. You have already become a ghost, which means you are not free. On the contrary, if you help me, not only would you be free, but you would also be able to roam with me." The ghost thought, "Today I am just so unlucky to be eaten by a tiger. For what reason must such bad luck fall on my head? I must find a person and let him suffer from being gnawed by a tiger. Moreover, the tiger is ferocious; if I cannot find another person for it, it will definitely not let me go." After contemplating, the ghost agreed to help the tiger find another person.

❸

Yúshì hún dàizhe lǎohǔ dào tā rènshi de yī
于是，魂 带着 老虎，到 他 认识 的 一

hù rénjiā Tā xiān ràng lǎohǔ duǒ zài yībiān ránhòu
户 人家。他 先 让 老虎 躲 在 一边，然后

zìjǐ guòqu qiāomén Tā qǐng zhǔrén chūlai gēn tā
自己 过去 敲门。他 请 主人 出来 跟 他

shuōhuà hái tuīshuō tiānqì hěn lěng xiǎng jiè zhǔrén de
说话，还 推说 天气 很 冷，想 借 主人 的

yīfu Zhǔrén suīrán bù tài yuànyì dàn zuìhòu háishi
衣服。主人 虽然 不 太 愿意，但 最后 还是

bǎ yīfu tuō xialai jiè gěi tā chuān le Zhège
把 衣服 脱 下来 借 给 他 穿 了。这个

shíhou lǎohǔ kàn chàbuduō le jiù tūrán pū chulai
时候，老虎 看 差不多 了，就 突然 扑 出来

chīle zhège rén Zhè yī cì lǎohǔ chī de hěn
吃了 这个 人。这 一 次，老虎 吃 得 很

A roaming ghost

48

痛快，因为 之前 魂 已经 想 办法 使 这个 人
脱了 厚厚的 衣服。 终于，老虎 饱 了，满意
地 拍拍 肚子，对 魂 说：" 好！ 你 以后
就 跟着 我 吧！ " 后来 大家 把 帮 坏人 害
别人，称为 " 为虎作伥 "，是 一 个 经常 用 的
成语。

Translation

❸   As a result, the ghost led the tiger to visit a family. He let the tiger hide on the side, and then went over to knock on the door. He asked the owner to come out and talked to him, saying that the weather was cold and asked the owner to give him some warm clothes to wear. The owner was not willing to do so but finally took his clothes off to give to the ghost to wear. At this moment, when the tiger saw that it was about time, it suddenly rushed out and ate the owner. This time, the tiger finished eating very quickly because the ghost managed to get the owner take his clothes off. Finally, after the tiger finished eating, it patted its belly with satisfaction and said to the ghost, "Well done, now you can follow and work with me!"

    According to the legend, there is a Chinese idiom wèihǔzuòchāng, describing a person who helps a bad guy to cause other people harm.

Looking for a Scapegoat

"Tì Sǐ Guǐ" is a Chinese folk legend that is often talked about; Chinese people would often use the term since it has become part of the everyday language.

In Chinese, "tì sǐ guǐ", is similar to "scapegoat" in English. When we say, "A person has become someone's scapegoat", we are referring that the latter, in order to avoid taking on his own responsibilities or to escape incrimination, would put the blame on the innocent former.

The story of "tì sǐ guǐ" came from ancient Chinese superstitions. According to belief, any person that had died from hanging, drowning, poisoning, labor complications, and other similar deaths, will become a wandering ghost, drifting aimlessly in the human world. It must haunt the place where it had died and find a substitute corpse. It will take possession of the body and pass its past faults to the soul of that particular body, allowing it to reincarnate and to be born into a new person.

In ancient times, ones that are often looking for "substitutes" are people who committed suicide by hanging, which are mostly sad wives and young brides. According to much of the stories, these "hanged ghosts" are usually women that are too worked up over a particular issue and just couldn't look at the brighter side.

In fact, not everyone that had perished would look for a scapegoat. According to legend, only an unjust individual would find someone else to replace himself. As for why they did not go and get revenge on those who had killed them, these legends have not given any reasonable explanation. Even more surprising is that these stories never took place at the same place, causing an endless cycle of people looking one by one for an authentic "scapegoat" story. However, even though there are many variations, Chinese people are not bored with these "tì sǐ guǐ" stories, even incorporating the term in everyday language.

GAMES FOR FUN

Match the following six tiger-related idioms (1–6) to their right explanations (a – f):

(1) 谈虎色变

(a) an encouraging statement to allow a person to feel strong and powerful

(2) 如虎添翼

(b) taking on something (or caring for someone) that will be harmful to you in the end

(3) 骑虎难下

(c) to use someone else's influence or power to bully other people

(4) 养虎为患

(d) to be scared when something horrible is mentioned

(5) 三人成虎

(e) to do something and want to quit halfway, usually because of fear

(6) 狐假虎威

(f) when a rumor was repeated enough, people would believe it like it is the truth

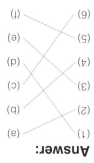

聂小倩
Niè Xiǎoqiàn

Nie Xiaoqian

Pre-reading Question

1. In Chinese legends, how do ghosts repay other people's kindness?

2. Have you seen a swordsman catching ghosts in Chinese movies?

---

❶ 宁采臣是一个书生。有一次，他要去办事，但在路上错过了可以住的地方，便在山上一座寺里休息。这座寺很清静，除了他这个客人外，南边的小屋还住了一个人。那晚宁采臣正要上床睡觉，一个女子突然走进来，笑着说："我住在北边的小屋，夜里

睡不着，想 来 陪陪 你。"他 听了 之后，立即
拒绝了 她。女子 十分 惭愧，很 快 便 离开
了。第二 天，一 个 人 带着 仆人 在 东边
的 房子 住，夜里 突然 死去。又 过了 一
夜，仆人 也 死 了。宁 采臣 有些 害怕，向
住 在 南边 小 屋 的 那个 人 请教，他 说 有
鬼 害 人。宁 采臣 认为
自己 没 做过 什么 坏
的 事，鬼 不 会 来
害 他，便 不 再
感到 害怕 了。

A scholar

Translation

❶   Ning Caichen was a scholar. He missed lodging on the way when he was traveling for business. As a result, he decided to stayed at a temple at the top of the mountain. This temple was quiet. There was another man staying in the small house on the south side.

When Ning Caichen was about to sleep at night, a girl came in. She smiled at him and said, "I live in the small house on the north side. I cannot fall asleep and so I am here to be with you." Ning Caichen looked serious and refused her. The girl was ashamed and left.

On the next day, a man came with a servant and lodged in the east wing-room of the temple. That very night he met his sudden death. The next night, the man's servant also died. Ning Caichen was a bit frightened. He asked the man in the south-wing room what had happened. That man said these men were killed by a ghost. Ning Caichen believed that ghosts would not harm him because he was an upright man who had done nothing wrong. Thus, he wasn't scared any more.

❷

到了 晚上，那个 女子 又 来到 宁 采臣 的 房间。她 对 宁 采臣 说："我 叫 聂 小倩，十八 岁 的 时候 生病 死去，埋 在 庙 旁。从此 以后，我 被 一 个 妖怪 控制着，要 替 他 寻找 男人 给 他 吃掉。现在 庙 里 已经 没有 可 杀 的 人 了，明天 晚上 妖怪 要 派 一 个 恶鬼 来 对付 你。你 是 一 个 好人，我 不想 害 你。你 必须 跟 住 南边 小 屋 的 那个 人 睡 在 一起，才 不 会 有 危险。"临 走 的 时候，小倩 又 说："我 实在 不 愿意 再 害 人 了。如果 你 能 带 我 的 骨头 离开，那个 妖怪 便 不 能 再 控制 我 了。"宁 采臣 很 同情 她，就

A temple

55

答应下来。第二天晚上，宁采臣来到南边的小屋，要求跟那人睡在一起。那人答应了宁采臣的请求。睡前，他把一个盒放在窗边。深夜时候，一个影子靠近窗户，想要进入屋内。忽然间，有一样东西从盒里跳出来，射中影子，立即又回到盒里，影子也消失不见了。早上，两人要离开这间寺了。住在南边的那个人原来是捉妖怪的剑客，分别之前，他送宁采臣一个口袋。宁采臣在庙旁找到小倩的墓，把她的骨头挖出来，装好后，便租了一条船回家了。

Translation

❷   At midnight, the girl came to Ning Caichen's room again and said to him, "My name is Nie Xiaoqiao. I died when I was eighteen years old and was buried near this temple. From then on, I have been controlled by a monster-like creature and have helped it seduce men who will then become its food. No one else was here to be killed now. Tomorrow night it will send a ghost to kill you. You are an upright man and I don't want to hurt you. You must stay with that man in the south wing-room to avoid the danger. Before she left, Nie Xiaoqiao said, "I did not want to harm any people again. If you can pick up my bones and carry them away with you, the monster-like creature cannot control me any more." Ning Caichen pitied her and he promised her to do so.

On the following night, Ning Caichen asked to stay with the man in the south-wing room. He consented to Ning Caichen's request to stay with him. Before he slept, the man put a box on the windowsill. About midnight, a dark shadow approached the window and wanted to get into the room. All of a sudden, something jumped out of the box and shot at the dark shadow. It returned to the box and the dark shadow disappeared.

On the next morning, the two of them were about to leave the temple. The man was in fact a swordsman who specialized in catching monster-like creatures. Before leaving, he gave Ning Caichen an old sack. Later, Ning Caichen found Xiaoqian's tomb. He dug up the bones, wrapped them up and brought them home by sea.

❸ Huíjiā hòu Nìng Cǎichén zhǎole
回家 后，宁 采臣 找了
yī ge shìhé de dìfang bǎ Xiǎoqiàn
一 个 适合 的 地方 把 小倩
de gǔtou mái le Zhè shíhou Xiǎoqiàn
的 骨头 埋 了。这 时候，小倩

A bone

biànchéng yī ge měilì de shàonǚ zhàn
变成 一个 美丽 的 少女，站
zài Nìng Cǎichén shēnbiān Tā shuō Wèile bàodá nǐ xīwàng
在 宁 采臣 身边。她说："为了 报答 你，希望
nǐ jiēshòu wǒ de qǐngqiú ràng wǒ liú zài nǐ de
你 接受 我 的 请求，让 我 留 在 你 的
shēnbiān yīshēng cìhou nǐ Nìng Cǎichén bèi tā de xīnyì
身边，一生 伺候 你。"宁 采臣 被 她 的 心意
gǎndòng le biàn dài tā huíjiā Guòle bùjiǔ liǎng rén hái
感动 了，便 带 她 回家。过了 不久，两 人 还
zuòle fūqī guòzhe xìngfú de shēnghuó Hòulái yǒu yī
做了 夫妻，过着 幸福 的 生活。后来 有一
tiān Xiǎoqiàn de shénqíng hěn bù'ān shuō Wǒ de xīn tiào
天，小倩 的 神情 很 不安，说："我 的 心 跳
de hěn lìhai kěnéng shì yāoguài yòu lái zhuā wǒ le Nìng
得 很 厉害，可能 是 妖怪 又 来 抓 我 了。"宁
Cǎichén shuō Bié pà wǒ shēn shang háiyǒu jiànkè sòng
采臣 说："别 怕，我 身 上 还有 剑客 送
de kǒudai ne Yúshì tā bǎ kǒudai ná chulai guà
的 口袋 呢。"于是，他 把 口袋 拿 出来，挂
zài mén shang Nà tiān wǎnshang Xiǎoqiàn zhèngzài wū nèi
在 门 上。那 天 晚上，小倩 正在 屋 内
zuòzhe Tūránjiān yī ge yāoguài shēnzhe shétou xiàng fēiniǎo
坐着。突然间，一个 妖怪 伸着 舌头，像 飞鸟
yīyàng xiàng Xiǎoqiàn pū guolai Zhè shíhou mén shang de
一样 向 小倩 扑 过来。这 时候，门 上 的

58

口袋 一下子 变 得 很 大，里面 探出了 一 个
鬼 一样 的 东西，把 妖怪 揪了 进去，口袋 也
恢复了 原来 的 模样。第二 天，宁 采臣 打开
口袋 一 看，里面 的 妖怪 已经 化成 水 了。

Translation

❸   When he returned home, Ning Caichen built a tomb and buried the bones of Nie Xiaoqian. At this moment, Xiaoqian turned into a beautiful young girl and stood near Ning Caichen. Xiaoqian said, "To repay your kindness, please accept my request to stay with you and serve you." Ning Caichen was moved by her sincerity and he brought her home. Some time later, they got married and lived happily together.

One day, Xiaoqian was very nervous. Ning Caichen asked her why. Xiaoqian said, "My heart is beating very fast. I guess the monster-like creature at the temple would come to get me." Ning Caichen said, "Don't be afraid. I had the old sack given by the swordsman. He took out the sack and hung it on the door.

That night, Xiaoqian was sitting in the house. All of a sudden, a monster-like creature stretched out its long tongue and attacked Xiaoqian. At this moment, the sack became very big and some ghost-like creature came out and dragged the monster-like creature inside. After that, the sack resumed its original size. On the next day when Ning Caichen opened the sack, the monster-like creature was turned into water.

Scholar

A scholar has a special status in Chinese history.

In ancient China, which kind of people can change their destiny the most easily? The answer is the scholar. If a scholar achieves good results in the government examination, he can become very successful and his social status will also change. Therefore, many scholars in ancient China were eager to become government officials in order to achieve their goal to serve the country and also because they can change their social and economic status.

Besides becoming officials, how can scholars make a living? For those who cannot become officials, they choose to teach. Confucius was the pioneer of the teaching profession. Scholars who have passed provincial examinations or had been local officials before were popular in the teaching profession. If the scholars do not achieve an outstanding result, their salary will be much lower. There is also a job called "Shi Ye" which is a member of staff in the government office. Their income is quite high.

If scholars do not want to work for an employer, most of them will sell their essays and portraits. In some prosperous areas, scholars can run their own businesses. Businessmen ranked the lowest in ancient China. But in Ming and Ching dynasty, the social status of businessmen has become higher and higher and a lot of scholars have changed their career and became businessmen.

GAMES FOR FUN

In the following pictures, please point out the image of a scholar in ancient China.

(1)

(2)

(3)

(4)

Huàpí

画皮

Painted Skin

Pre-reading Question

1. What weapon would a Taoist priest used to kill a demon?

2. Have you heard of *the Strange Stories of Liaozhai*?

---

❶ Wáng Shēng shì yī ge shāngrén Yǒu yī tiān tiān méi
王 生 是 一 个 商人。 有 一 天, 天 没

liàng tā jiù chūmén le Zài lù shang tā kàndào qiánmian yǒu
亮 他 就 出 门 了。 在 路 上, 他 看到 前面 有

yī ge shíjǐ suì de shàonǚ yě zài lù shang zǒu Nàge
一 个 十 几 岁 的 少女 也 在 路 上 走。 那个

shàonǚ zhǎng de hěn měilì què mǎnhuái xīnshì Wáng Shēng kuài
少女 长 得 很 美丽, 却 满怀 心事。 王 生 快

zǒu jǐ bù zhuīshangle tā gēn tā biān zǒu biān liáo Wáng
走 几 步, 追上了 她, 跟 她 边 走 边 聊。 王

Shēng zhè cái zhīdao yuánlái shàonǚ de fùqin jiāng tā mài
生 这 才 知道, 原来 少女 的 父亲 将 她 卖

gěi yī ge yǒuqián rén zuò xiǎolǎopo Dànshì nàge rén de
给 一 个 有钱 人 做 小老婆。 但是 那个 人 的

dàlǎopo měitiān dōu dǎmà tā tā shízài shòubuliǎo jiù
大老婆 每天 都 打骂 她, 她 实在 受不了, 就

逃 出来。王 生 很 同情 她，忍不住
说："你 不如 到 我 家 住 一 段 时间，再 想
办法 吧。"少女 想了 一下，很 快 便 答应
下来。王 生 把 少女 带 回 家 后，不想 给
妻子 知道，就 安排 少女 住 在 后院 的 房间
里，晚上 还 偷偷 过去 跟 少女 睡觉。

Translation

❶ Wang Sheng is a businessman. One day, he traveled before daybreak. He met a teenage girl who was also in hurry to get somewhere. This girl was beautiful but she seemed to be worrying about something. Wang briskly walked a few steps to catch up with her and both had a conversation as they are walking. Wang soon found out that the girl's father had sold her to a rich man as a mistress. The wife of the family would curse at her every day. Unable to stand it anymore, the young girl had decided to flee from the family. Wang pitied her. He could not help saying, "You could live with me for a period of time and think about what to do next." The girl thought it over and then quickly agreed to the proposition. Wang brought the girl home but he did not want his wife to know. So he arranged for the young girl to live in the room at the back of his house. He would sneak to sleep with the girl at night.

❷
Jǐ tiān hòu Wáng Shēng zhèngzài shìchǎng zuò
几 天 后， 王 生 正在 市场 做

mǎimai bèi yī ge dàoshi lāzhu le Dàoshi shífēn
买卖， 被 一 个 道士 拉住 了。 道士 十分

jīngyà de shuō Nǐ de shēntǐ shàng xià yǐjing bèi guǐ
惊讶 地 说："你 的 身体 上 下 已经 被 鬼

de xiéqì bāowéi le Zuìjìn nǐ shìbushì yùdàole
的 邪气 包围 了！ 最近 你 是不是 遇到了

shénme qíguài de shìqing Wáng Shēng jiānjué de shuō
什么 奇怪 的 事情？" 王 生 坚决 地 说

méiyǒu dàoshi zhǐhǎo yáozhe tóu zǒu le Huí jiā hòu Wáng
没有， 道士 只好 摇着 头 走 了。 回家 后， 王

Shēng láidào fángjiān fāxiàn mén dǔshangle zěnme yě
生 来到 房间， 发现 门 堵上了， 怎么 也

dǎbukāi Yúshì Wáng Shēng zǒu dào chuāng qiánmian wǎng lǐmiàn
打不开。 于是， 王 生 走 到 窗 前面 往 里面

kàn zhè yī kàn què bǎ tā xià ge bànsǐ Yuánlái fángjiān
看， 这 一 看 却 把 他 吓 个 半死。 原来， 房间

lǐmiàn yǒu yī zhī lǜsè de èguǐ ér chuáng shang zhèng
里面 有 一 只 绿色 的 恶鬼， 而 床 上 正

The skin of the young girl

放着一张少女的人皮，恶鬼正拿着笔在人皮上画着什么。过了一会，恶鬼画好人皮，就像穿衣服一样把人皮穿在身上，变成了那个漂亮的少女。王生吓坏了，马上去找那个道士。道士见他实在可怜，就给他一把拂子，让他回去之后挂在门上。王生回到家里，再也不敢进房间去。晚上就睡到另一间房间里，还把拂子高高挂在门上。半夜，那少女来到门口，看到拂子，就停住了，不敢靠近，很生气的样子。过了很久，少女终于作了决定。她一把抓下拂子，把它撕得粉碎，然后踢开门闯进房间去，直冲到王生的床上，用她的手指一挖，把王生的心挖出来，然后便离开了。

Translation

❷   A few days later, Wang Sheng was in the market buying goods and was stopped by a Taoist priest. The Taoist priest was very surprised and said, "Your body is completely surrounded by the aura of evil ghosts! Have you been experiencing anything unusual recently?" Wang Sheng firmly denied. The priest had no choice but shook his head and left. After returning home, Wang Sheng went to the room where the girl was staying. He found the door to be locked and he was unable to find a way to open it. As a result, Wang went to the window and took a look inside; from what he had seen, it had almost scared him half to death. In the room was a green-faced demon, and on the bed laid the skin of the young girl. The evil demon was holding a brush and painting over the human skin. In a minute, the demon finished painting the skin. Just like putting on clothes, the demon simply put on the human skin and became the beautiful girl.

Wang Sheng was terrified and immediately went to the Taoist priest. The Taoist priest pitied him and gave him a brush-like tool, which could be hung on the door. Wang Sheng went home and dared not to return to the room again. At night, he slept in another room and hanged the brush-like tool high on the door. In the middle of the night, the young girl came to the door and saw it. She stopped and dared not come any closer. After a long time, the girl finally made the decision. She grabbed the brush-like tool, tore it to pieces and kicked open the door. She went straight to Wang Sheng's bed, ripped out Wang's heart with her claws, and left.

❸

第二天，王生 的 弟弟 发现 哥哥 死在 床 上，马上 去 通知 道士。道士 愤怒地 说："我 本来 想 放过 她，想不到 这 恶鬼竟然 这么 大胆。"于是，他 跟着 弟弟 来到王 生 的 家，却 发现 那 少女 已经 离开 了。

道士 向 周围 看了 一下，说："她 跑 得 不远，到 南边 的 房子 去 了。"弟弟 吃了一 惊，说："南边 的 房子 是 我 的 家啊！"弟弟 带着 道士 来 到 南 院，刚 进家门，弟弟 的 妻子 便告诉 他，刚刚 来了 一个老 妇人，想 当 他 家 的工人。道士 说："就是那个 女 鬼 了。"说完拿出 剑，站 在 院子中间，大 喊 道："女

A Taoist

guǐ Kuài bǎ fúzi huán wǒ Lǎo fùrén jiàn xíngshì
鬼！快 把 拂子 还 我。"老 妇 人 见 形势

bùmiào gāng xiǎng táozǒu dàoshi jiù chōngle shàngqù zhuī dǎ
不妙，刚 想 逃走，道士 就 冲 了 上去，追 打

nà lǎo fùrén Lǎo fùrén bèi dǎ de diē
那 老 妇 人。 老 妇 人 被 打 得 跌

zài dì shang shēn shang de rén pí diàole
在 地 上，身 上 的 人 皮 掉了

xiàlái mǎshàng biànchéngle yī zhī nánkàn de
下来，马上 变成 了 一 只 难看 的

èguǐ tǎng zài dì shang xiàng zhū yīyàng
恶鬼，躺 在 地 上 像 猪 一样

jiào Dàoshi náqi mùjiàn yīxià jiù bǎ
叫。 道士 拿起 木剑，一下 就 把

èguǐ de tóu kǎnle xiàlái Nà èguǐ
恶鬼 的 头 砍了 下来。 那 恶鬼

lìjí biànchéng nóngyān dàoshi náchu yī ge
立即 变成 浓烟，道士 拿出 一 个

A bottle gourd

húlu bǎ nóngyān quánbù shōu jìn lǐmiàn
葫芦，把 浓烟 全部 收 进 里面。

Translation

❸   On the following day, Wang Sheng's younger brother found his brother dead in bed and immediately sent for the Taoist priest. The Taoist priest said angrily: "I wanted to leave her alone but I did not expect her to be so immoral." So he went to Wang Sheng's home with his brother only to find that the girl had left. The Taoist priest looked around and said, "She has not run too far away; she is at the south court." Wang Sheng's brother was taken aback and said: "The southern side is my home!" Wang Sheng's brother went with the Taoist priest to the south court; as they entered the house, his wife told him that an old woman had just dropped in and wanted to be his house servant. The Taoist priest said, "That is the female demon!" Taking out a wooden sword, he stood at the middle of the yard and yelled: "Demon! You had better quickly give me back my tool!" When the old woman saw that the situation was getting dire, she tried to escape. The Taoist priest rushed up and ran after the old woman. She was beaten to the ground until her human skin fell off, immediately turning into an ugly demon and howling like a pig. The Taoist priest picked up the wooden sword and with one strike, cut down the head of the demon. The demon then became a pile of evil smoke. The Taoist priest took out a bottle gourd that absorbed all the smoke.

Strange Stories of Liaozhai

"Strange Stories of Liaozhai" is a masterpiece from Pu Songling. Liao Zhai is the name of his bookstore; however it is also known for a different reason, which is being usually associated with strange stories. It is said that Pu Songling opened a teahouse in front of his home and asked each patron to share stories with him; if the story happens to be well told, the patron would not have to pay for his tea. Because these stories have provided such a wealth of materials, with further editing and processing, the book became what it is now.

As Qing Dynasty's most famous collection of short stories, this work contains 491 short stories. Most of these stories are weird tales about fox-demons, immortals, ghosts, and demons; these stories are rich in content, bizarre plots, twists and turns. The most fascinating part is that the collection is not simply made up of common plots about struggles between humans and ghosts; it is also made up of plots about humans and fox-demons, humans and spirits/gods, as well as romantic love stories between two people. The stories' protagonists, whether they are fox-demons, ghosts, mistresses or poor scholars, are willing to fight against destiny and face death unfalteringly for their pursuit of unwavering love.

In the world of Pu Songling's stories, humans are depicted as ugly and ignorant; not only are they greedy, selfish, ruthless, but they are also hypocritical. On the contrary, fox-demons ghosts are shown to have strong characters. Although many of them are intentionally harmful at heart, some of they are depicted as passive, kind-hearted and grateful. Not only are they not harmful but they would sometimes also save lives. In order to keep a promise or in order to pursue love, they would even sacrifice their own lives. It is these different fox-demons and ghosts that cause these Liao Zhai stories to make such an impact to the hearts of the Chinese people, making them such popular stories to this very day.

GAMES FOR FUN

You have already read about these characters in the book. Can you match their identity with (a) – (d)?

(1)	Baogong	(a)	a judge
(2)	Bai Sujing	(b)	snake demon
(3)	Ziyu	(c)	a princess
(4)	Zhong Kui	(d)	a ghost catcher

Answer:
(1) — (d)
(2) — (a)
(3) — (b)
(4) — (c)

É lóng

鹅笼

The Goose Cage

Pre-reading Question

1. Can you tell the difference between a Chinese duck and a goose?

2. Have you ever seen any pictures of Chinese Xians (Immortals)? How are they different from fairies in the West?

---

❶

Yǒu yī ge jiào Xǔ Yàn de rén zài shān li zǒu Tā
有 一 个 叫 许 彦 的 人 在 山 里 走。他

shǒu li tízhe lóngzi lǐmiàn zhuāngle yī duì é Zài
手 里 提 着 笼 子，里 面 装 了 一 对 鹅。在

lù shang tā yùjiàn yī ge dàyuē
路 上，他 遇 见 一 个 大 约

shíjǐ suì de qīngnián Qīngnián shuō
十 几 岁 的 青 年。青 年 说

zìjǐ de jiǎo yǒu diǎn tòng qǐngqiú
自 己 的 脚 有 点 痛，请 求

Xǔ Yàn ràng tā jìnrù lóngzi bù
许 彦 让 他 进 入 笼 子，不

xiǎng zìjǐ zài lù shang zǒu Xǔ
想 自 己 在 路 上 走。许

A goose cage

71

Yàn xiǎng tā zài kāi wánxiào, shuí zhīdao lóngzi de mén yī
彦 想 他 在 开 玩笑，谁 知道 笼子 的 门 一

kāi nà qīngnián jiù jìnqu le Qíguài de shì qīngnián
开，那 青年 就 进去 了。奇怪 的 是，青年

yǔ yī duì é zài yīqǐ nà
与 一 对 鹅 在 一起，那

lóngzi méiyǒu biàn de dà qīngnián
笼子 没有 变 得 大，青年

yě méiyǒu biàn de xiǎo é yě
也 没有 变 得 小，鹅 也

méiyǒu hàipà Xǔ Yàn tíqi
没有 害怕。 许 彦 提起

lóngzi juéde bìng bú zhòng
笼子，觉得 并 不 重 。

A goose

Translation

❶   There was a person called Xu Yan walking in the mountains. In his hands, there was a cage; and in the cage, there was a pair of geese.

     On the road, he met a young man in his teens who said his feet hurt and requested Xu Yan to let him crawl into the cage so he did not have to walk. Xu Yan thought the young man was joking. However, when he opened up the cage, the young man crawled into the cage. Strangely enough, the cage itself had not grown any bigger when both the young man and a pair of geese were inside. The young man did not shrink and the geese showed no fear. When Xu Yan picked up the cage again, the cage was light in weight.

❷ 许彦来到一棵大树下休息，青年从笼子里出来，对许彦说："我想请你吃一顿饭，表示感谢。"许彦说："很好。"于是，那青年从嘴里吐出一个盘，盘上有饭有菜。两个人喝了一些酒，那青年对许彦说："这些日子，有一个女人跟着我；我想暂时把她叫出来。"许彦说："很好。"于是青年从嘴里吐了一个美丽的女人出来，大约十多岁，还跟他们一起喝酒。不久青年醉了。那女人对许彦说："我虽然爱这个青年，可实际上偷偷带着一个男人。青年既然睡了，我想暂时把这个男人叫出来，希望你不要告诉他。"许彦说："好吧。"于是这女人便从口中吐了一个男人出来，大约二十岁，也十分

聪明。不久，青年快醒来了，美丽女人吐了一个屏风出来，她到屏风后面，和青年一起睡。那男人对许彦说："这个女人虽然爱我，但我还偷着约了一个女人来，现在想见她。希望你不要把这些事情告诉这女人。"许彦说："好的。"于是，这男人又从口中吐了一个二十岁左右的女人出来。

Translation

❷ Xu Yan rested under a tree and the young man came out of the cage and said to Xu Yan, "I want to treat you to dinner to express my gratitude." Xu Yan said, "Fantastic!" Afterwards, a tray came out from the teenager's mouth and on the tray there was food.

Both parties drank some wine and finally the young man told Xu Yan, "In these few days, there was a woman with me and right now, I want to make her appear." Xu Yan said, "Alright." From the young man's mouth came a very beautiful woman and she joined them in drinking wine.

Moments later, the young man was drunk and the woman said to Xu Yan, "Even though I am in love with the young man, I am also in love with another man. Right now, I want to make this man appear. I hope you won't tell the young man." Xu Yan said, "OK." From the woman's mouth came a 20-year-old man who was very smart. Moments later, when the young man was about to wake up, the woman spat out a folding screen and went to sleep with the young man behind the screen.

Then the 20-year-old man said to Xu Yan, "Even though I am in love with this woman, there was another woman in love with me and I want to make her appear now. I hope you won't tell this to the previous woman." Xu Yan said, "Sure." From the man's mouth, came a 20-year-old woman.

❸ 过了好长时间，屏风内有声音，男人说："他们已经醒了。"于是将所吐的女人吞进口中。不一会儿，那个美丽女人从屏风后面出来，对许彦说："青年快起来了！"然后将那男人吞进口中。青年起来后，对许彦说："我睡得太久了，让你一个人坐着，真对不起。天已经很晚了，要跟你告别了。"青年说完，便将那女人和所有盘都吞进口中，只留下一个大的盘送给许彦，青年向许彦告别说："分别后，我们只有互相想念了！"

后来许彦看见盘上面有字，写着是公元一世纪做的，是三个世纪之前的东西。

Translation

❸   After a long time, there was sudden movement behind the screen. The man said, "They have woken up." Then, the 20-year-old woman was swallowed back into the man's mouth.

Soon the beautiful young woman came out from behind the screen and said to Xu Yan, "The young man is about to wake up very soon!" Then, the young man was swallowed back into the beautiful young woman's mouth.

"The young man woke up and said to Xu Yan," "This sleep has just lasted too long and caused you to sit here all by yourself. I am really sorry about that. It's getting late and I must say goodbye to you." Once the young man finished talking, the young woman, the cups and bowls were all swallowed back into his mouth, leaving only the big tray to Xu Yan. The young man said goodbye to Xu Yan, "We must part now. However, we can only reminisce about one another from now on."

Later, Xu Yan saw that on the big tray there were actually characters stating the tray was actually made during the 1 AD, three centuries before Xu Yan's time.

China's Xian / Immortals

To put it simply, a "xian" is an immortal. "Xian" stories appeared at the same time when Chinese Taoism was introduced and developed; of all of the stories, the most popular story is the story of the Eight Immortals.

Tie Guai Li 铁拐李 (Iron-Crutch Li) is the leader of the Eight Immortals. He was originally a very cultured and good-looking man. He once used Taoism to allow his spirit leave his body so he can travel thousands of mils away to listen to a speech given by an enlightened individual. Unexpectedly, his ignorant disciples thought he had died and burned his body. His spirit came back and cannot find the body; he had no choice but to crawl into a beggar's body that was located in the vicinity. He inherited the beggar's appearance: dirty, ugly, and also lame in his right foot. By this time, he had already attained immortality. By using his own saliva, he can turn a bamboo in his hand into a crutch made of iron.

During the Tang Dynasty, there was a person called Han Zhongli 汉钟离. His poetic verse "Often sitting and lying with a pot of wine" accurately depicts the image of Zhongli Quan, an immortal by the same name, of the Eight Immortals.

Zhang Guo Lao 张果老 (Elder Zhang Guo) is the eldest of the Eight Immortals. He has a habit of riding a donkey backwards for thousand of miles for a day.

Of the Eight Immortals, Lü Dongbin 吕洞宾, who is slender, tall, learned and charming, is the most in touch with humanity.

He Xiangu 何仙姑 (Immortal Woman He) is the only female in the Eight Immortals. She is often holding a lotus. Legend said that when she was 13-years old, she ate a divine peach, which caused her to be no longer hungry or thirsty, to be able to fly, and to be able to predict the good and bad fortunes in life.

Lan Caihe 蓝采和 is often depicted as a happy tramp, dressed in a worn-out blue gown. In his hands, there will be a pair of bamboo castanets, which he would use to create a beat while he sings and dances. He would randomly sing songs about what he had seen in his environment but because his songs are related to the surroundings, they would usually have underlying meanings.

Han Xiangzi 韩湘子 is a young man who is exceptionally good with the bamboo flute.

Cao Guojiu 曹国舅 is often holding a jade plaque, which he had used when he was a royal official with the government.

"Xian" stories usually share the same beliefs that exist in Taoism. Much of the stories are about those that do not seek fame and fortune, and pays more attention to self-improvement while doing good deeds, regardless of being able to achieve immortality, longevity, happiness, respect and love.

GAMES FOR FUN

Identify the Eight Immortals in the picture show below.

(1)   (2)   (3)   (4)

(5)   (6)   (7)   (8)

Answer:

(1) Zhang Guo Lao   (2) Lan Caihe   (3) Han Xiangzi   (4) Cao Guojiu

(5) Lü Dongbin   (6) He Xiangu   (7) Tie Guai Li   (8) Han Zhongli

Bái shé zhuàn

白蛇传

The Legend of the White Snake

Pre-reading Question

1. Snake is a symbol of the Devil in the West. Do you think snake also symbolizes evilness in the Chinese culture?

2. There is a belief that a man has another life before he is born. Imagine what you would do in this life before you were born.

---

❶

Xī Hú shì Zhōngguó hěn piàoliang de hú nàli yǒu
西湖是中国很漂亮的湖,那里有

yī zuò tǎ zhè zuò tǎ yǒu yī ge dòngrén de gùshi Hěn
一座塔,这座塔有一个动人的故事。很

jiǔ yǐqián yǒu yī ge niánqīngrén jiào Xǔ Xiān yī tiān tā
久以前,有一个年轻人叫许仙,一天他

chéng chuán yùjiànle měilì de Bái Sùzhēn Zhè shíhou tiān
乘船遇见了美丽的白素贞。这时候,天

tūrán xiàqǐ yǔ lai Xǔ Xiān jièle zìjǐ de sǎn gěi
突然下起雨来,许仙借了自己的伞给

tā Cóngcǐ yǐhòu liǎng gè rén jīngcháng jiànmiàn Shíjiān
她。从此以后,两个人经常见面。时间

cháng le liǎng gè rén mànmàn chǎnshēngle gǎnqíng Hòulái liǎng
长了,两个人慢慢产生了感情。后来,两

人 结婚，生活 得 很 快乐。 许 仙 继续 在
药店 里 工作； 他 的 妻子 就 给 附近 的 人
治病，并且 不 收 费用。 但是，他们 的 做法
影响了 附近 一 座 寺，因为 病人 都 不 愿意
再 去 那里 寻找 帮助，这 使 寺 里 的 和尚 很
生气。

Translation

❶   Xi Hu is a beautiful lake in China. At the lake is a pagoda where a touching story took place.

    Long time ago, there was a young man called Xu Xian. He happened to meet Bai Suzhen when he was traveling by sea. At this moment, it suddenly began to rain and Xu Xian lent her his umbrella. Since then, Xu Xian and Bai Suzhen saw each other very often. As time went by, they fell in love. Some time later, they got married. After being married, they lived a very happy life. Xu Xian continued to work in an herbal medicine store while his wife cured local people of their diseases free of charge.

    But their actions slowly affected the business of a nearby temple as fewer and fewer sick people were willing to seek help there. The temple's monk became very angry.

❷

和尚 为了 报复，就 告诉 许 仙，他 的 妻子 是 蛇变 的。 许 仙 不 相信，和尚 告诉 他，端午节 的 时候，大家 会 喝 药 酒 来 防止 生病，白 素贞 喝了，就 会 变成 蛇 的 样子。 许 仙 在 端午节 的 时候 骗 他 妻子 喝 这 种 酒。 他 妻子 喝了 之后，难受 得 不得了，躺 在 床 上 睡着 了。 许 仙 回到 房间，看见 床 上 躺着 一 条 白 蛇。 他 很 害怕，就 这样 被 吓死 了。 白 素贞 醒来 后 很 伤心，她 到 天上 偷了 药，救活了 丈夫。 白 素贞 向 丈夫 承认 自己 是 蛇 变 的，她 跟 他

結婚，是 为了 感谢 他 曾经 救过 她，现在 她
jiéhūn shì wèile gǎnxiè tā céngjīng jiùguo tā xiànzài tā

已经 有了 他 的 孩子。 许 仙 知道 后，虽然
yǐjing yǒule tā de háizi Xǔ Xiān zhīdao hòu suīrán

仍然 感到 害怕，但是 接受了 这个 事实。
réngrán gǎndào hàipà dànshì jiēshòule zhège shìshí

Translation

❷   To get revenge, the monk told Xu Xian that his wife was actually a thousand-year-old snake demon. Xu Xian was doubtful. The monk told him that his wife would only reveal its true self by drinking a special kind of herbal wine on Tuen Wu Festival. Xu Xian managed to deceive his wife to drink this wine on Tuen Wu Festival. After drinking the alcohol, his wife felt sick and went to bed. Coming back to the room, Xu Xian saw a white snake sound asleep on the bed and he was actually scared to death.

Bai Suzhen woke up to find her husband dead. She flew to the Heavenly Palace to steal an immortal herb and revived her husband. Bai Suzhen admitted to her husband that she was indeed a thousand-year-old snake demon. To thank him for having saved her, she had married him and was now bearing his child. Xu Xian still felt a bit frightened but he decided to accept this fact.

❸ 和尚 知道 两 个 人 又 在 一起 之后，就 想 办法 骗 许 仙 到 寺 里，不 让 他 回 家。白 素 贞 很 愤怒，救了 丈夫 之后，用 水 淹了 那 座 寺。后来，和尚 趁 白 素 贞 生下 儿子 不久，身体 弱，捉住 白 素 贞，把 她 压

A tower

在 西 湖 边 的 一 座 塔 下面，永远 不 能 出来。经过 这 件 事，许 仙 很 灰心。他 在 塔 的 下面 生活，照顾 儿子，同时 保护 妻子。后来，他们 的 儿子 长大 了，在 全国 考试 中 取得了 第一 名。他 来到 塔 前面 看 母亲 的 时候，打败了 和尚，把 母亲 从 塔 下面 救 出来。许 仙 一家人 经过 无数 困难，终于 可以 在 一起 生活 了。

Translation

❸   When the monk knew that the couple had reconciled, he decided to lure Xu Xian to the temple and kept him from home. Bai Suzhen was furious and rescued her husband before flooding the temple. Not long after Bai Suzhen gave birth to her son, the monk seized Bai Suzhen when she was weak and confined her under a pagoda at Xi Hu, unable to be freed ever again.

Xu Xian was so desolate that he became a monk at the pagoda. He looked after his son while accompanying his wife at the pagoda. Later, their son grew up and was able to achieve the first place in the government examination. As he was going to the pagoda to pay respect to his mother, he managed to defeat the monk, rescuing his mother from the pagoda. After countless twists and turns, Xu Xian and his family are finally together again.

West Lake's Legend of the White Snake (Leifeng Pagoda, Broken Bridge)

The Broken Bridge is one of West Lake's most famous bridges. Its name is closely linked with the folklore "Legend of the White Snake". The White Snake and Xu Xian actually met each other at the Broken Bridge when they are heading back to the city in the same boat and exchanged the umbrella as a token of love; later, they have reconciled with each other again at the Broken Bridge. In the "Legend of the White Snake", the White Snake is a cute being. She is a demon and is also a god; however being a demon and also a god is not what she really wants. She just wants to be normal. She just wants to be a normal person, enjoy ordinary love, and live a normal life. It is precisely because of her desires and ideas that made her a legendary figure. This also makes the "White Story Legend" a story of endurance.

Today, the Broken Bridge was rebuilt in 1921 as a single-arched stone bridge. "Melting Snow on Broken Bridge" is one of West Lake's top ten sceneries and is part of West Lake's unique winter landscape. One side of the Broken Bridge faces the city while the other side faces the mountain; during the early spring, if you were standing on Gem Mountain overlooking at the Broken Bridge, you would see snow in the melting phase. On the sunny side, the scenery of "Melting Snow, Collapsing Bridge" would appear; while on the darker and snow-capped side, the scenery of "Broken Bridge Unbroken" would appear.

The Leifeng Pagoda, in a sense, gained an outstanding reputation precisely because of the trapped White Snake. But in fact, we already know that Leifeng Pagoda and the White Snake is actually irrelevant. Built in 975 AD, the emperor of the Wuyue Kingdom built it as a celebration of the birth of his son. It is also West Lake's iconic attraction. Whenever the sun sets behind the tower's horizontal open spaces, by creating a unique scenic attraction, this became known as the origin of the term "Leifeng Afterglow".

GAMES FOR FUN

From the three images shown below, which woman is playing the role of Bai Suzhen?

(1)

(2)

(3)

Jú xiān
菊仙
Chrysanthemum Fairies

Pre-reading Question

1. What other ways do you think chrysanthemum can be used besides decoration? Have you seen them in Chinese food or drinks before?

2. A kind of animal is often transformed into spirits in Chinese ghost stories. Can you guess what it is?

❶

Cóngqián yī ge xìng Mǎ de jiātíng yīzhí hěn rè'ài
从前，一个姓马的家庭一直很热爱

zhòng júhuā Dàole Mǎ Zǐcái zhè yīdài tā duì zhòng
种菊花。到了马子才这一代，他对种

júhuā de rèqíng gèng shēn le Yǒu yī tiān Mǎ Zǐcái zài
菊花的热情更深了。有一天，马子才在

dàichéngshì mǎile liǎng kē hǎnjiàn de júhuā pǐnzhǒng Huíjiā
大城市买了两棵罕见的菊花品种。回家

de lù shang Mǎ Zǐcái yùjiàn yī wèi shàonián tā qízhe
的路上，马子才遇见一位少年，他骑着

lú gēn zài yī liàng chē de hòumian Mǎ Zǐcái biàn gēn tā
驴跟在一辆车的后面，马子才便跟他

聊起来。少年知道马子才热爱菊花的事情后，两个人谈了很久。少年说："要养好菊花，品种并不重要，最要紧的是种的方法。"马子才问起了他离开大城市的原因，他说："你看！前边车上坐着的是我姐姐。因为姐姐在大城市住不惯，我带着她到别的地方去住。"马子才问："你们决定到哪里没有？"少年回答："还没有！我们走到哪里，就住在哪里吧！"马子才提议他们住到自己家里去，他说："虽然我不是富有的人，但有几间房子，到我家住吧。"少年没有立即答应，走到车的旁边，问姐姐的意见。姐姐说："房间不用太大，只希望有大些的院子。"就这样，两个人就到马家住下了。"少年把马子才扔掉的菊花烂枝拾回家，重新培育，他照顾的院子长满了漂亮的菊花，很多人到他那里买花，生意做得越来越好，少年赚了不少钱，房子也盖得越来越漂亮。

Translation

❶   Once upon a time, the Ma family are known for their love for chrysanthemum flowers. This strong love for chrysanthemum was passed from generation to generation to Ma Zicai.

One day, Ma Zicai traveled to the big city for two branches of unusual chrysanthemum species. He met a young man riding a donkey behind a chariot. Ma Zicai began chatting with the young man. When the young man knew that Ma Zicai was a chrysanthemum lover, they began to share with each other even more. "For chrysanthemum, it is not the species that matters, the key lies in how you plant them," the young man said. When Ma Zicai asked why he left the big city, the young man said,"You see, the lady in the chariot is my sister. The big city does not suit her so we are moving to other places." "Have you decided where to stay?" asked Ma Zicai. "Not yet, we can stay wherever we go," he replied. Ma Zicai suggested that they could stay at his place. "Though I am not a rich man, I have a few cottages. You can stay with me if you don't mind," he said. Instead of accepting the invitation immediately, the young man went towards the chariot to ask if his sister liked the idea. "The cottage doesn't need to be big, if only it has a spacious courtyard," she said. They finally settled down at Ma Zicai's place. Later on, the young man brought home the rotten chrysanthemum branches dumped by Ma Zicai and planted them in the courtyard. Under his care, the branches bloomed with beautiful blossoms attracting flocks of people to buy flowers from him. The planting of chrysanthemum turned into a profitable business. The young man earned a lot and his cottage became a luxurious one.

❷

Guòle sān nián Mǎ Zǐcái de tàitai shēngbìng
过了 三 年, 马 子才 的 太太 生病

sǐqu Mǎ Zǐcái qǔle shàonián de jiějie Yī tiān Mǎ
死去, 马 子才 娶了 少年 的 姐姐。 一 天, 马

Zǐcái péi shàonián hē jiǔ Tāmen hēle hěn duō jiǔ zuì
子才 陪 少年 喝 酒。 他们 喝了 很 多 酒, 醉

de lián lù dōu zǒu bù zhí le shàonián zài huí jiā de lù
得 连 路 都 走 不 直 了, 少年 在 回 家 的 路

shang jīngguò júhuā dì bù xiǎoxīn dǎo dì jiù biànchéngle
上 经过 菊花 地, 不 小心 倒 地, 就 变成了

jùdà de júhuā gēn rén chàbuduō gāo kāizhe shíjǐ
巨大 的 菊花, 跟 人 差不多 高, 开着 十几

Blooming chrysanthemums

朵拳头大的花。马子才吓得要死，赶快去告诉少年的姐姐。她急忙跑来，把菊花从地里拔出放在地上，说："怎么醉成这样？"第二天早上，马子才去看少年，发现他躺在地上，睡得很香，才知道姐姐和弟弟两人都是仙。过了一段时间，少年又喝醉了，又倒在菊花地里。马子才这次不奇怪了，拔出菊花。没想到过了不久，菊花渐渐失去了生气。姐姐知道后，跑来一看，吓得大叫："你害死我的弟弟啦！"她把其中一段根带回家，小心照顾，菊花终于活了过来。到了秋天，那支根开满了发出酒香的花。如果用酒来浇花，花就长得更加茂盛了。

Translation

❷   Three years later, Ma Zicai's wife died from illness. He then married the young man's sister. One day, Ma Zicai and the young man drank together. They drank a lot. The young man was so drunk that he was unable to walk properly. On his way home, he passed the chrysanthemum fields. Tripped by some flowers, he fell into a field and immediately turned into a giant chrysanthemum that is as tall as a man and blossoming with fist-big flowers. Scared to death, Ma Zicai hurried to tell the young man's sister about this. His sister ran to the field, pulled out the chrysanthemum and laid it on the ground. She said:"How come you become so drunk?" The next morning, when Ma Zicai went to the field, he found the young man in a deep sleep on the ground. He then realized that both the two of them were chrysanthemum fairies. Some time later, the young man was drunk and fell into the chrysanthemum field again. No longer shocked this time, Ma Zicai plucked out the chrysanthemum as his sister had done before. Unexpectedly, it withered after a while. When his sister knew this and rushed to the scene, she was terrified. "You killed my brother!" she screamed. She brought home a section of its root, planted it into the soil and took good care of it with patience. In autumn, the root bloomed with flowers scented of wine. If irrigated with wine, this flower would bloom even more attractively.

Spirits in China

Demons, monsters and goblins appear in many different forms in the West. The most familiar ones include satyrs which are half man and half goat in Greek and Roman mythology. They have different natures and characters. Some are righteous while others enjoy causing trouble. Some look ugly while others look lovely. In contrast, most of the spirits in China are evil. The idea of spirits is used to rationalize unexplainable natural phenomena or mysterious power. Spirits in China are neither gods nor human beings. They are creatures that possess supernatural power.

In general, animals and plants experience a transformation process to become spirits. If the animals and plants were kind-hearted during their transformation, they would become mortals. If they were evil, they would become evil spirits. Spirits often appear in the form of human beings and pose threats to mankind.

There are a lot of Chinese legends about spirits. The fox spirit is one of the most famous ones. Fox spirits are often in disguise as beautiful young ladies who deceive young gentlemen and take their lives. A famous title, Strange Tales of Liaozhai, written by Pu Songling contains many stories on fox spirits.

GAMES FOR FUN

Orchid, bamboo, chrysanthemum and Chinese plum are symbols of "Four Virtuous Men" in Chinese culture. Can you identify each of them in the following pictures?

(1)

(2)

(3)

(4)

Glossary

Common Words and Phrases			HSK Rank	Page
àidài	爱戴	popular	Adv	01
ànjiàn	案件	cases	Adv	37
bànlǐ	办理	handle	Adv	01
bàodá	报答	an expression of gratitude	Adv	4
bàofù	报复	get revenge on	E / I	82
bāowéi	包围	surround	E / I	64
bùjuéde	不觉得	did not feel	E / I	01
cǎn	惨	unlucky	E / I	47
cánkuì	惭愧	ashamed	E / I	53
chéngyǔ	成语	idiom	E / I	4
chǒulòu	丑陋	ugly	Adv	01
chuánshuō	传说	legend	E / I	30
chūmén	出门	on the road	E / I	62
chúxī	除夕	New Year's Eve	Adv	33
cìhou	伺候	serve	E / I	58
cōngmíng	聪明	smart	E / I	74
dǎn	胆	guts	E / I	22
dàoqiàn	道歉	apologize	E / I	9
dēnghuǒ	灯火	candle light	E / I	01
diàn	殿	palace	Adv	30
dīxià	低下	be nobody	Adv	01
dízi	笛子	bamboo flute	Adv	30
ēn	恩	gratitude	Adv	01
é	额	forehead	Adv	36

E / I = HSK Elementary / Intermediate Level
Adv = HSK Advanced Level

fēnbié	分别	farewell	`E / I`	9
fěnsuì	粉碎	tear sth to pieces	`E / I`	65
fǒurèn	否认	deny	`Adv`	01
fūqī	夫妻	husband and wife	`E / I`	18
gāoshàng	高尚	of high virtue	`E / I`	01
gōngláo	功劳	contribution	`E / I`	3
guānyuán	官员	official	`Adv`	14
hàoqí	好奇	curious	`E / I`	9
héshang	和尚	monk	`Adv`	84
huáiyí	怀疑	suspicious	`E / I`	25
huàjiā	画家	painter	`E / I`	33
huángjīn	黄金	gold	`Adv`	01
húlu	葫芦	bottle gourd	`Adv`	68
jiānyù	监狱	prison	`E / I`	41
jiǎrú	假如	if	`E / I`	1
jìmò	寂寞	lonely	`E / I`	17
jīngyà	惊讶	surprised	`E / I`	64
júhuā	菊花	chrysanthemum	`Adv`	87
kàojìn	靠近	approach	`E / I`	56
kòu	叩	knock on	`E / I`	01
lǎopo	老婆	wife	`E / I`	1
lěngjìng	冷静	keep cool	`E / I`	23
língqián	零钱	small change	`E / I`	01
lóngzi	笼子	cage	`E / I`	74
lúnliú	轮流	take turns	`E / I`	24
mǎchē	马车	chariot	`Adv`	01

`E / I` = HSK Elementary / Intermediate Level
`Adv` = HSK Advanced Level

màoshèng	茂盛	bloom attractively	Adv	92
míxìn	迷信	superstitions	E / I	44
mù	墓	tomb	E / I	11
nǚzǐ	女子	a young lady	E / I	55
ǒurán	偶然	by chance	E / I	7
pǐndé	品德	virtue	E / I	01
píngfēng	屏风	screen	Adv	76
pū	扑	jump out	E / I	48
púrén	仆人	servant	Adv	11
qǐngjiào	请教	ask	E / I	53
qīngxǐng	清醒	out of one's mind	E / I	2
quántou	拳头	fist	E / I	92
shāngrén	商人	businessman	E / I	62
shàonǚ	少女	young girl	E / I	7
shēnqíng	深情	deep emotion	Adv	19
shíjī	时机	opportunity	E / I	01
shǒuhù	守护	protect	E / I	01
sì	寺	temple	Adv	52
sīniàn	思念	miss	E / I	17
sǐxíng	死刑	a death sentence	Adv	41
táozǒu	逃走	escape	Adv	68
tūn	吞	swallow	E / I	76
wǎnglái	往来	contact	E / I	16
xiǎobiàn	小便	urinate	E / I	39
xīnyì	心意	wish	E / I	20
xiōng'è	凶恶	ferocious	E / I	44

E / I = HSK Elementary / Intermediate Level
Adv = HSK Advanced Level

xūruò	虚弱	weak	E / I	01
yánlì	严厉	serious	E / I	01
yānmò	淹没	flood	Adv	01
yāoguài	妖怪	monster-like creature	Adv	59
yīngjùn	英俊	handsome	Adv	01
yòngxīn	用心	take good care of sth	E / I	01
yù	玉	jade	Adv	14
zhòngzhí	种植	plant	E / I	01
zhuǎ	爪	claws	Adv	01
zhùshǒu	助手	assistant	E / I	41
zhǔyi	主意	idea	E / I	24
zuòzhàn	作战	at war	E / I	3

E / I = HSK Elementary / Intermediate Level
Adv = HSK Advanced Level